THE GREAT CANADIAN ANECDOTE CONTEST

THE GREAT CANADIAN ANECDOTE CONTEST

Edited by George Woodcock

Introduced by George McWhirter

HARBOUR PUBLISHING

Published by
HARBOUR PUBLISHING
P.O. Box 219
Madeira Park, BC Canada V0N 2H0

Cover watercolour *Toni painting on Cheakamus Glacier, 22 October 1983* by Toni Onley, used with kind permission of the artist

CANADIAN CATALOGUING IN PUBLICATION DATA

Main entry under title:
The great Canadian anecdote contest

ISBN 1-55017-058-9

1. Anecdotes—Canada.   I. Woodcock, George, 1912–
PS8365.T34 1991   C818'.5408   C91-091674-8
PR9197.9.T34 1991

CONTENTS

AN EDITORIAL NOTE

After the great success of its Canadian Poetry Contest in 1987–88, Canada India Village Aid decided to launch in the fall of 1991 a competition in the neglected art of anecdote. Apart from the competitors who submitted their entries to us (and whose best fifty anecdotes, including those of the six prize winners are here included), we invited a group of professional Canadian writers to submit guest anecdotes that would be *hors concours*, and considerably more than half the invitees (the twenty-one represented here) responded.

The contest was organized on behalf of CIVA by a committee consisting of George Bowering, Patricia La Nauze, George McWhirter, George Woodcock and Ingeborg Woodcock; they also served as the primary reading committee and selected the works to go to the final judges. These were Silver Donald Cameron, the Maritime journalist and writer; George Galt of *Saturday Night*; Vicky Gabereau, the CBC radio host; and Alan Twigg, editor of *BC BookWorld*.

We thank all these patient participants, so generous with their time. We also thank Margaret Atwood for her example in preparing *Barbed Lyres*, an anthology resulting from a satirical contest on behalf of *This Magazine*,

9

whose general format we found an excellent model and have shamelessly imitated.

We are grateful to all the participants, competitors and guests, who have allowed their anecdotes to be reprinted here without royalty on behalf of Canada India Village Aid. The proceeds will be used for village rehabilitation, training health workers, and environmental rehabilitation in some of the poorest parts of India. Finally, we express our thanks to Howard White of Harbour Publishing for bringing out this anthology, to Toni Onley for offering a cover drawing, and to all the magazines and other media outlets that publicized our venture.

—GEORGE WOODCOCK

George McWhirter

INTRODUCTION

Not unexpectedly, the idea for "The Great Canadian Anecdote Contest" came up at a dinner party, where so many such stories are shared. Goh Poh Seng—a medical doctor and writer from Malaysia, now living in Canada—and his wife, Margaret, were telling of an accident on a road in Ireland. George and Inge Woodcock, my own wife (Angela), David Watmough and Floyd St. Clair all began to tell of their near misses. This anthology, then, is an invitation to join the company, and perhaps the stories should not be read but listened to—in that spirit—with a glass of whisky in good company and a readiness to add your own story to the pot.

Although the contributors are arranged by name, alphabetically, it isn't uncommon to find that sequences of accident on the road stories develop; also serious, supernatural encounters with dead people, animals, and birds abound, or you may run into a silly but sobering one with a kangaroo. Many stories turn on the misunderstanding of a word, or the understatement of something outrageous. There are contortions and adventures in strange lavatories. In fact, the places we repair to in our hours of need—home, bed, hospitals, restaurants—all come with crises and stories attached.

Because anecdotes are told when people are at ease,

unexpected information is often divulged. Here we learn about a prank one of our best-known writers has played on poor unwitting sleepers at summer camp, and that another scribe, famed and beloved for inflammatory rhetoric, actually sets places on fire in a certain part of the US simply by passing through.

Coincidence is the mother of these narratives, and the unexpected twist is at the very navel of their successful delivery.

All of us collect anecdotes to retell; we imagine ourselves being interviewed on radio or entertaining a room full of friends with them—new stories for old friends, old ones for the new. In this sense, the Canada Village Aid anthology is only a single offering in a tradition that will go on for as long as people have tongues to tell what odd things happened to them on their way to meet with us for dinner.

THE ANECDOTES

Athena Paradissis

TULIPE NOIRE

Tulipe Noire wasn't her birth name. Her baptismal certificate read Amy Smith, but Amy Smith conjured images of aimless smithereens and in theatre, aimless smithereens conjured images of obscurity so she adopted the name Tulipe Noire, pronounced the français-from-France way.

Tulipe was in love. This was not unusual. "I was born in love," she would explain to new acquaintances while gently stroking Ara Pacis beneath his chin. Ara Pacis was her cat whose namesake, an ancient Roman ruin, meant altar of peace. That the "dear" Prince of Pacification assumed a prerogative to execute every creature that moved, did not diminish his mistress's adulation. "He has spirit," she would retort to those who dared question her constant patronage of Johnson & Johnson Band-Aids.

Her latest passion, a well-known actor named James, had humbly given her an autographed photograph.

"His face looks as if it's about to fall off," I observed.

"What do you mean?"

"Look at his chin—it's practically touching his knees."

"He is a man of experience—it's called character."

"How old is he?"

"Sixty."

"Then it's called old age."

Call it what you would, it didn't discourage her obsession even though it was clearly unrequited. "It's just a phase of his," she would offer by way of commentary—to which she later added, "he is in love with me only he hasn't yet realized it." Anyway, just as it seemed that he would never get over this phase and that the great revelation would never strike, Tulipe decided that intervention by seduction would awaken James to his desires. So, wearing a sexy black bustier with attached garters, she put on her oversized Columbo raincoat and explained "Operation How-To-Hook-A-Hunk"—"I am going to follow him in the car, secretly, and then surprise him at his front door."

"But you don't drive," I contested.

"True," she conceded, "but you do."

That night we followed him, with the headlights turned off, and everything was going according to the James Bond Sensuous Spy Scheme until BANG! CLATTER! SPURT!—right into the rear bumper of a police car, also undercover and, consequently, also without headlights. To the station they took us whereupon one of the officers, suspicious of Tulipe's oversize columbocoat, asked her to take it off. Well, imagine their surprise when she complied!

"Name?" asked the officer in command.

"Amy Smith," Tulipe replied, and then she flashed her girl-next-door smile because sometimes, obscurity is the best thing that you can hope for.

PRIZE

Robin Bridgman

HARRISON LAKE PICNIC

In the fall of 1978, when the kids were quite small, Toby seven and Jennie five, I decided on a whim to drive the whole family to Harrison Lake. The dog, of course, had to be included.

The sun was shining, but it was cold. It was a lovely drive, and before long we were all on the pebbled shore of Harrison Lake, throwing stones, running up and down and generally having a good time. I felt the water in between throws, just because I had a good skipper. Yikes that was cold, it reminded me that the lake was glacier-fed.

We built a small three-stone fire and roasted our hot dogs. It was as I was taking a bite out of my second hot dog that my son Toby suddenly interrupted our conversation by saying, "Daddy, the dog is swimming but he's not moving!"

I cast my eye out at the dog, about a hundred yards from the shore. He was a duck-tolling hound, just a fancy name for a dog that likes to retrieve anything from the water. I had last seen him diving for stones. I had to agree. The dog was paddling hard but not moving. I called his name, but no change.

"Daddy! Daddy! Copper will drown!" came the shrill voice of one of the children.

I looked around for a log that I could sit on to paddle—but there was nothing quite so big. There was not a kayaker, fisherman or boater in sight.

"I'm sorry kids, but the water is far too cold to swim in. I'm afraid we'll have to leave him for the moment and drive to Harrison to get help."

"But that's too far away! He will drown by the time we get back!"

"I'm not swimming out there and that's that! Have you felt the temperature of that water?" I turned to see their upturned, angelic faces. I knew right then that if the dog died they would never trust me again.

I stripped down to my shorts and dove into the water. It was a mistake. Most of the air in my lungs exhaled in a whine. Desperately I struck out for the dog. As I approached, I could see him smiling. I came up on him quickly, wishing firstly that I had swum that fast at school and secondly that I had left the dog there and gone for a boat.

I freed his leg from a forked branch that lay just under the surface and the two of us headed for the shore. By now I couldn't feel my feet, and my hands were numbing. Never mind, we'll soon be on the shore. I watched my lovely wife run to the car for one of our big blue beach towels. Her blond hair played in the sun as she ran back to the beach, to dry me. However, she ran right on by, with the children, to comfort the dog.

PRIZE

Hume Compton

WHAT'S IN A NAME?

The view from the treetop is clear enough to see the shell bursts. Speaking into the radio, he directs the gunners' aim a few degrees. A new sighting shot is fired. He picks up the microphone to confirm—and his world blows up. A Japanese mortar has exploded on contact with a neighbouring tree. Riddled with shrapnel, he falls to the ground—completely oblivious to what has happened to him.

The infantry platoon, laboriously working its way through the dense Burmese underbrush, comes upon the wounded soldier. He's quickly, but gently, carried back to the company's front-line base. Other platoons probe forward, stumbling, sweating, cursing. Somewhere out there are the forward elements of the enemy, looking for weak spots. This time the Japanese find some, and push forward. The British fall back.

Gunner Douglas Compton from London (via Scotland), of the Royal Artillery, seriously wounded, receives rudimentary first aid, and is placed on a cot in the forward dressing station. There are over a dozen cots, all occupied. He's the only one not belonging to the front line infantry.

Suddenly, there's wild yelling. Bullets stutter and zing in all directions. The position is overrun. The British retreat farther, firing as they back up into the jungle. They are forced to leave the wounded behind.

Japanese soldiers swarm into the forward base vacated by their enemy. They are jubilant with their small victory, but know it could be temporary. They set up a squad beyond the tents, waiting for the counterattack which they know will come, probably at first light in the morning.

They rampage through the primitive base—smashing radios, gathering food and water, salvaging weapons and ammunition. A squad enters the first-aid tent and discovers the wounded, lying in two rows of cots down the sides of the tent.

An officer shouts an order, and soldiers rush through the tent, plunging bayonets into the deathly still bodies.

A company of the King's Own Scottish Borderers counterattacks, and in a running fire-fight the Japanese are pushed out of their recently captured position. The Scottish regiment hadn't waited for dawn. They knew there were wounded left behind when the others retreated.

There isn't much left of the forward position by the time the Jocks secure their hold. The first-aid tent, however, with its large red cross painted on its roof, is still intact, hiding its grisly contents.

An anguished shout comes thundering out of the tent, through the open flaps. The atrocity has been discovered—the dead bodies silent witnesses to the frantic brutality of the retreating Japanese.

A soldier is assigned the harrowing task of recording the names of the victims from the identification disks hanging round their necks. One by one the names go into his little notebook. None of them are from his regiment—they are strangers to him.

He comes to the Royal Artillery spotter, an odd-man-out among the infantrymen. He reads "D. B. Compton." I went to school with Doug Compton, he says to himself, not too common a name. He turns the body over to see its face. He recognizes him immediately as his old schoolmate.

This is unbelievable, he thinks. He looks closer. Did he see a movement in an eye? Can he be alive? Yes, yes, he is!

He tears out of the tent, shouting for the medical orderly—anyone. He spots an officer. Grabs him by the arm and splutters out that one of the bodies is alive—and he knows him—went to school with him! He's almost incoherent.

Gunner Compton had indeed been bayoneted, but had only received a flesh wound on his side. He's totally unaware of what has happened—and how close he has come to death. He is still close to death, however, from his earlier wounds.

He's quickly evacuated, passed through several hands, and finally reaches India, where he spends nearly a year in a military hospital near Bombay.

He survived. During his convalescence he used his time in creating what was reputed to be at that time India's largest English language library. Pandit Nehru, soon to become India's first prime minister, came to open it.

He's a retired schoolteacher now, living in East Anglia, England. He spends a lot of his time fishing, hiking and birdwatching.

My brother's life was spared by a little fibre name tag—by an old schoolmate intrigued by the name he found on it.

PRIZE

R. Lee Rose
MISSED MOOSE

One crisp autumn afternoon, I decided to go for a walk in the woods beyond our home. As moose-hunting season was open, I picked up the rifle, and thereby inspired the participation of my four-year-old son, Robbie. So, with him sitting on my shoulders, and the rifle tucked under my arm, I began a pleasant excursion down an abandoned logging road.

I had not expected to actually see a moose so close to the house, when a hulking antlered form rose up from a patch of browning fireweeds near the top of a sloping meadow to my left. Realizing that he would not have moved unless he sensed my approach, I also realized that I had not much time to get off a shot before he went over the rise and disappeared into the forest.

Without even pausing to take Robbie from my shoulders, I quietly worked the bolt to load a round into the chamber. The moose looked at me curiously when the bolt clicked shut, but did not turn away. I lined up the open sights for a perfect neck shot. I couldn't miss. But, I did.

I quickly ejected the spent round while the moose turned and began walking up the hill waggling his ears like berserk radar antennas at the sounds behind him. I got off another shot at his receding rump, and one more just before he disappeared over the top.

Perhaps he would stop on the other side and pause

to look back before going into the woods. If I could get up the hill quickly enough, I might get one more chance. I ran up the hill gasping for air, with Robbie bouncing on my shoulders like a bareback rider, until at last I could see over the rise. Sure enough, the moose stood at the edge of the forest, gazing back. My hands shook as I loaded a fresh round, and tried to steady my aim. I held my breath, gently squeezing off my last shot.

Just before the rifle kicked, the moose wheeled, and vanished into the willows. I had missed again, and knew that none of my other shots had done any better.

Despairing, I stood Robbie on the ground and kneeled beside him to catch my breath.

Clearly pleased by the exciting diversion, Robbie put his hand on my shoulder.

"I saw a moose, Daddy. Did *you* see him?"

PRIZE

Jeanette Howat

A WHALE OF A TALE

There are many stories that we Maritimers like to tell. Pull up a chair and I'll warm your heart with a tale that fascinates me to this day.

My partner Cyril and I had fished the Atlantic for many a year, and we knew the unpredictableness of the sea and its creatures. We were inshore fishermen by trade, and the sea was in our blood; we ate it, we slept it, we lived it, but we had never seen, before or since, what we saw that day.

We had been out in our dory for three hours, pulling up nets that had been set the day before. We had almost finished when we spotted something lying on the top of the water, one hundred yards away. It was a blow top, and I could tell by its markings that it was a humpback. At first glance I guessed that it was forty feet long, three times the size of our dory.

Humpbacks are usually playful, but this one was unusually still. We cut our motor and coasted near to it. I could see that it was entangled in one of our nets. That happens often at sea—us and the whale wanting the same fish. We knew that it would die if it stayed the way it was.

We drew closer, so close that I could look into its eye. I had never seen that look before. It was as if it was asking for help. My heart went out to it and I knew that I had to help this fellow creature.

As we pulled our boat alongside, it didn't move. A whale that big could easily capsize our dory. We were nervous, for you see, oldtimers like us never learned how to swim, nor did we wear lifejackets. We saw that from the boat we couldn't cut the net from the animal's back. It was then that Cyril had the idea to get out and walk on the whale.

We cautiously stepped out onto it. It was dry and not slippery. We crawled along to its head and began cutting. The whale didn't move at all. We were afraid that once the net loosened it would take off like a shot, leaving us to fend for ourselves in its wake. We worked our way down its back and the whale still remained motionless.

Holding our breath, we got back in the boat and waited to see what it would do. Amazingly, it swam slowly away from us, still on top of the water. It seemed to know that if it made a sudden move, it would capsize us. At fifty yards it dove deeply beneath the water, with its white-bottomed tail in the air. I still think of that as its farewell and adieu to Cyril and me.

We sat motionless for a while, thrilled that our plan had succeeded. With enough excitement for one day, we headed to shore, eager to tell our tale back home.

PRIZE

Eric Stofer

MY MOTHER'S OFT UNRELATED TALE

When I was a strip of a lad, my mother frequently reminisced about her life as a young girl, growing up in Edwardian England.

One of her favourite tales concerned bedbugs.

Bedbugs were an affliction in every English household then, when feather beds were commonly used—the Royal Household and the bed of the reigning monarch no exception. This gave rise to a lively service trade in which, for a few shillings, those engaged in the practice would rid your beds of bugs. Naturally, such tradesmen became known to the locals as "buggers."

Two such tradesmen opened shops on the same street, near Tottenham Court in London, where my mother lived; the shops were directly across the street from each other, which made locals wonder since the proprietors had identical surnames.

The two tradesmen soon became rivals, in stiff competition to service local households, with neither outwardly revealing animosity toward the other . . .

Until, one day, one of those tradesmen was summoned to service the Royal Household—and the bed of the King.

Apparently the man did his job well, for besides rewarding him generously, the Sovereign granted the man permission to display, on his shop above his name, an elegant Royal Coat of Arms together with the inscription: "Bugger to His Majesty the King."

This the proud tradesman promptly did.

Beneath that, however, apparently in an attempt to clarify matters as well as emphasize his new status among his peers, he scrawled the following: "No Relation to the Bugger Over the Road."

BY INVITATION

Margaret Atwood
CAPERING

The year, if you can imagine it: 1959. A more naive year than this, when thrills were cheaper.

I was nineteen, and working as the Nature and Campcraft instructor at an Ontario summer camp called White Pine (where sun will always shine). In practice, this meant identifying squashed caterpillars and stepped-on mushrooms, and teaching small boys to light fires with one match. This last made me very popular. I was also a member of the Trip Staff, which meant that I took out canoe trips on which the small boys made Kraft Dinner and then wet their sleeping bags.

White Pine was a co-educational Jewish camp, run by a man named Jo-Jo Kronick, who was something of a kibitzer himself, and took on the entire male staff every summer in a ketchup-and-mustard squeeze-bottle fight in the dining room; so he could hardly object to the occasional prank pulled by the staff on one another. The only rules were: i) no murders, and ii) the campers were not to be involved. This made the Trip Cabin fair game: the male Trip Staff slept there, all by themselves.

The heads of departments were known by their professions. I was Peggy Nature, and Beryl Fox (later to work on "This Hour Has Seven Days" and to make the astonishing Vietnam documentary *The Mills of the Gods*) was Beryl Horses; that is, she ran the riding program.

She also had a reputation for being slightly reckless. I on the other hand am a cautious person, so—I protest—it was she who tempted me, and not the other way around.

Beryl's ambition was to pull a flawless caper on the Trip Cabin. After much planning, here is what we did.

In the dead of night, we tiptoed into the Trip Cabin. As my colleagues blissfully snored, we glued all their shoes to the floor. We then filled them full of horse manure, and covered the door handle with shaving foam. We spread more manure on the porch; after this, we climbed up onto the roof and jumped up and down. When we judged that the occupants of the cabin were fully awake and about to come after us, we skinned down off the roof, ran back to our own cabins and jumped into bed. Meanwhile, the Trippers were trying to put on their shoes, failing, grappling with the slithery door handle, and running out onto the manure-covered porch in their bare feet.

Shortly an annoyed posse of them made the rounds of likely suspects, asking questions and inspecting rubber boots for tell-tale signs of night excursions. I had taken the precaution of wiping my boots off, and I do a great wakened-from-slumber crabby act. No one was arrested that night, but the next day, as I was teaching yet more small boys how to light fires with one match, I heard a scream and a splash. The Trippers had decided Beryl's guilt, and had rubbed a raw egg into her hair and thrown her into the lake.

As for me, my air of nerdish innocence saved me, as it has done on later occasions. I was never caught.

Now you know, folks: it was me, all along.

Steven Berry

A SURPRISING MOMENT IN EUROPE

I was atop the Leaning Tower of Pisa, disoriented by the sloping spiral stairs and the absence of guardrails, irritated by two girls scratching their names into the bell, and I was waving to Sylvie, my travelling partner, on the ground. She didn't notice.

The sun behind me caused the edge of the tower's shadow to fall right across her blanket, so I swung my arms crazily, so she might see the shadow move and look up.

No luck. I was about to give it up and go read the bell when a man approached her. Sylvie's method of discouraging unwanted male attention is to make no response, so the man answered his own question and sat down.

He asked other things, but Sylvie—the stoic—made like he wasn't there. Which aggravated him . . . he touched her shoulder. She pulled away. He put a finger to her chin, turning her head . . . It was all too much for me.

From my position on the Leaning Tower of Pisa, the sun distorting my compact form into that of a flaming god, I let out a tumultuous roar—"YOU! GET AWAY!"— and in the quiet Italian afternoon, my war cry echoed from buildings all around.

My position on the tower gave me another advantage. The man could withdraw at an easy pace, with his pride, which the whole time seemed to be the issue.

It was not until we met a Montrealer on a train to Barcelona that events coincided.

Discussing methods for dealing with unwelcome attention, I described to him what had happened in Pisa, holding that Sylvie's silence was not a good defence, and that she'd be better off acting insane.

I would have gone on to suggest impersonations of chickens and mules as effective, but at that very instant the wind from the window blew an insect into my eye and up under my eyelid! Panicked, I grabbed a bottle of spring water and began slopping it onto my face.

When I'd dislodged the kamikaze bug, the man from Montreal was staring at me. I explained myself.

"Oh," he said. "I thought this was a demonstration."

BY INVITATION

George Bowering
THE RAIN BARREL

When I was eleven years old my parents and I spent a lot of the summer fruit season on a big orchard in Naramata. It was so big that it was called a fruit ranch. My uncle managed this place and lived in one of the houses on it. At the northeast corner of this house there was a rain barrel. It didn't rain very often in the Valley, but you could depend on a deluge to damage the cherry crop, and maybe another terrific downpour in peach season. In between there might be an early morning shower from time to time.

But everyone who lived on an orchard ten miles from the nearest real town had a rain barrel. They knew where to put them to get nearly all the rain that hit the roof. Women liked to wash their hair in rain water because the regular water in the Valley was full of minerals. You couldn't make the softest soap lather up.

An eleven-year-old boy does two things with a rain barrel. On cloudy days he sticks his head in and yells for the marvellous echoes. On bright sunny Valley days with puffy white clouds he looks at the reflections of the puffy white clouds. We could stay in the past tense. These were the things he did in the days before boys watched television, which was slow to get to the Valley, but which now controls the imagination there, with moving images of the mean streets of Detroit. And that person is a long way past eleven years old.

One day that boy was watching the puffy clouds slide over the surface of the water, when all of a sudden the reflected sky was filled with the huge shaggy head of God.

He turned and looked behind him. He looked above him. He decided to look in every direction. He could see tractor smoke rising from between the trees fifteen rows to the west, but no human beings.

He looked back into the rain barrel. There was God's face again, maybe closer than the clouds, maybe just bigger than the clouds.

Then he was in the water, face first. Grabbed by the ankle and tipped in. A prince struggling to get back out. In his kicking and underwater yelling he made it harder than it need be, but he got out, all wet in the good morning sun.

He looked around again, and saw his uncle with his normal friendly creased face and grin, carrying something that needed fixing. He was just coming out the kitchen door of his house.

The eleven-year-old boy looked carefully at his uncle's face. It did not at all resemble the reflected face of God. He looked at the water again. It was still rippling, so any reflection was just a little plane of chaos.

He decided to wait until the water became a simple mirror again. But a squall brought in dark low clouds from the east, and soon it was raining into the rain barrel. Next thing he knew his mother was telling him to get in out of the rain. What could I do? When I was eleven years old my mother's word was law.

Lily E. Breland

DEAR JOHN

Public washrooms were created by sadistic woman-haters to torment the unsuspecting soul when caught in a vulnerable position. The cubicles look harmless enough, standing straight and tall, like an honour guard, but it doesn't seem to matter which one I pick, there's always something wrong with it.

The other day I was shopping when the strong urge from nature helped me find the women's public facilities in a hurry. As I was most impatient to relieve myself, I was not discerning in my choice. I grabbed the first available cubicle and poured myself in. I soon found I had entered the twilight zone of toilets.

A fast visual check showed me there was no hook on the back of the door for my purse. No problem—I'll just hold it in one hand while I squat to do my business. I couldn't possibly rest the purse on the floor—some kid might reach under the eighteen-inch gap between the walls and the floor and make off with my five-dollar canvas special.

Years ago, I was instructed by well-meaning persons never to fully sit down on public facilities as you never know what that porcelain throne has seen. So—I'm concentrating on keeping two inches of space between me and the germ giver, when I notice the door on my cubicle standing slightly ajar. Great! No lock—now what do I do? After all, I can't have a two-year-old poking his head in and learning the facts of life from my half-naked body.

I jam one foot up on the door as there's still that eighteen-inch gap to cover. So, there I am—teetering two inches off of the seat, my right arm up in the air with a death grip on my purse and one foot crammed in the door.

What should have been a quiet communal with nature has suddenly turned. I'm in a carnival horror house and I never even had to pay admission.

I blindly reach with my left hand underneath my right arm for sheets of wipes to dry off with and find nothing but empty metal hooks! The drip dry method should only have to be used after rinsing your hands.

Leaning against the door to pull up my bunched articles of clothing, I realize I've probably had more exercise here than running a mile. I know now how Chinese contortionists have learned to turn themselves inside out. At least they get paid for what they do—I barely got relief!

Bob Buckie
THE DELHI MAIL

The overnight Calcutta–Delhi express jerked to a halt in a small, nameless town outside of Patna. As the setting sun cast long brown shadows, I took the opportunity to stretch my legs and sip *chai* from a tiny earthenware cup. Twenty carriages of eight compartments; at least six people to a compartment, I tallied. Over a thousand people, about half now milling about on the platform.

Weaving purposefully through this crowd, a young Indian dressed neatly in flannels, white shirt and a thin V-neck cricket sweater made his way toward me. "Good afternoon, sir," he introduced himself, shaking my hand. "My name is Kumar." Without waiting for a reply he continued, "You are Canadian. You have come from Kathmandu, returning to Delhi. Do not go there. Go instead to Majestic Hotel in Varanasi. They will ask twenty rupees but say you will pay only ten."

With that he left.

"How the hell did he figure that out?" I wondered. There were no tell-tale maple leaves, no labels; my bag was Indian-made, my accent was Scottish; if anything, I looked German or Scandinavian after my rather severe haircut. But I knew already not to question anything in India. So, heeding his advice, I broke my journey and sought out the Majestic, demanding half the asked-for price.

A knock came and Kumar appeared. "In Varanasi I am your guide. Very cheap. Tomorrow, we will hire a rowboat. Dawn is best time to see Ganges," he stated laconically and disappeared once more. We did not see the sun rise, however, as there was a terrific thunderstorm. "Quite auspicious," he observed, drawing on his student knowledge of Victorian literature.

The Ganges was peculiarly devoid of people and the churned water a dark khaki. As he pulled on the oars, Kumar insisted that the water was quite drinkable. This, I did question. He did show me unusual aspects of this most remarkable city, for which I gratefully added a little bonus, but it was time to get back to the Guptas in New Delhi.

"*Booki-ji*!" Gupta shouted on my return. "Where have you been? We were so worried."

"Sorry about that, Mr. Gupta, but I can look after myself, you know," I protested. He thrust the previous day's newspaper at me, the headlines blaring: DELHI-MAIL CRASH. 7 KILLED, 84 INJURED.

Gulp!—my train. Auspicious indeed, Kumar—almost suspicious.

Vanessa Clift
SPIRIT OF DIRECTION

People often talk about the great influences in their lives. I listen and never speak—until now. I couldn't see that Joe Average next to me on the couch at a cocktail party, could understand.

One of my two influences is dancing. Sounds common enough, I know. Many people are born with a talent, whether they play with it or not.

I wasn't born to dance, or so I thought. Sure, I took the occasional lesson. I was given a little tutu and pretty pink satin shoes, and ballet classes to match. I was told they were good for me but I took no notice.

In fact, I took no notice of anyone or their advice. Except trends. So when I was thirteen, I joined a new dance school 'cause I liked myself in spandex catsuits. Occasionally, I got a large part in one of their shows, and loved the attention, as well as the small sweat droplets along my spine.

My teacher was elegant and cool, so I sometimes listened to her. One day she told me of an audition, and I agreed.

It started off another unpromising rainy Monday. I could hear drops plinking on the skylight as I trembled in front of the panel of old men. Then I noticed the bongo drummer.

His fingers were padding lightly across the skin, waiting for me to start my routine. Then the beat became stronger, exhilarating. I whirled around, smooth as honey. Sunlight was falling through the skylight onto his face, while everything else was rain.

Then I saw another face, similar to his, glowing in

37

the ray. Another pirouette, and the drummer was alone again. I gasped.

After my piece, I went over to ask him about what I had seen. I was awkward from amazement. I thought he wouldn't believe me.

"No, that doesn't sound stupid. Of course not. I'm glad you saw him. That's my twin brother who died a few years ago. We were very close . . ."

But I'd stopped listening to him. I was, instead, listening to a part of me that guides, that scorns neither my own ideas, nor other people's. My spirit of direction.

Now, when I hear about other influences, or their disbelief in something special, my mind wanders to that day, and I am free to be silent.

Mairead Coid
TEA LEAVES

The war was over and my eldest sister, a big blonde, was in love again. They had released the German POWs from the camp and allowed them to wander along the beach while they were waiting for repatriation. Eric, a tall, blond Squaddie with ice-blue eyes, was the subject of Eldest Sister's infatuation. The more the family and the neighbours disapproved, the more she adored him. They were a magnificent pair.

She had her teacup read. The tea leaves were not for tall blondes. "You will marry a short, dark foreigner and you will die in a hot southern land," said the fortune teller.

"Not me," said Eldest Sister and gazed out the window at the cold, grey Irish Sea and the windswept beach where her Eric might walk.

But Eric went back to Hamburg, and my two sisters went to London and many dances. At one, a short, dark foreigner asked Middle Sister to dance. She was also short and dark, so they made a dainty pair. The foreigner returned Middle Sister to her seat, where he met Eldest Sister. They fell in love and married. Later, they emigrated to Canada and lived seven years in Ottawa until the tea leaves had their way.

He was offered a contract in South America. Seven years later, they moved to the South Pacific.

My eldest sister is still married to the short, dark foreigner, and they live in the south of Spain.

BY INVITATION

John Robert Colombo
YOU GOT THE WRONG MAN

Writers receive the oddest mail. Nestled amid the bills, there's sometimes a gem to be found.

Here's a gemstone that arrived in a plain white envelope with no return address. It was handwritten in capital letters with a ballpoint pen on lined paper.

March 4th '91

Mr. Columbo,

Sir, I just bumped into you at Becker's (Bedford R.), Approx. 1 hr. ago. I asked you if you were Mr. Columbo [*sic*], and you denied being he.

Maybe I didn't wear a shirt & tie & wasn't worth talking to, Sir. I seldom wear a shirt & tie but I make more in a year than you do in a lifetime.

I am doubly upset because I always approved of your journalistic views. You don't pussyfoot around & [you] call the shots as they are.

There is no hope for this town, and now even John Robert Columbo is a fucking flake.

With respect to your query re the vandals & thieves at Beckers. Yes . . . *30* punks raided the place, & they were all *Blacks* but we can't give those "stats" can we in Toronto [?]. Surely not in the Toronto Star.

It's your town fellows 'cause I and thousands of others are leaving, but next time own up to your name!

R. Sanders

P.S. Peter Falk you certainly aren't!

That's Mr. Sanders's letter. Here's my own reply.

6 March 1991

Dear Mr. Sanders:

I double-checked my calendar pad. I was nowhere near Becker's on that day. I'm seldom on Bedford Rd. You accosted somebody else and accused him of being *me*.

I'm always surprised to be recognized by readers and I always chat with people who say hello. I don't know what you mean about punks raiding the place.

Some people say that I look like the actor Al Waxman or like the late Paul Rimstead, the columnist. (I don't see any resemblance myself.) Maybe it was Al you saw. It certainly wasn't Paul or me.

I know I'm no Peter Falk. And from your own account of the way you were dressed, you're no George Sanders.

You got the wrong man. Join the RCMP. They always get theirs.

John Robert Colombo

Diana Daly
A TIME OF INNOCENCE

During the 1920s, the Pacific Great Eastern Railway ran in and out of the residential area close to the shoreline in West Vancouver, to North Vancouver.

This episode occurred in 1924 near Altamont in West Vancouver.

Jimmy and I had a project. We were going to build a lighthouse. I was seven and Jimmy was eight.

"We need sand for cement," said Jimmy. He was more knowing than I 'cause he was older. "We'll put rocks on the PGE tracks and the train will crush them into sand."

"Oh, oh! Like the time we laid some of my dad's nails on the track and the train flattened them? They looked like little spoons and knives!" I was catching on.

We worked feverishly until we heard the none-too-distant rumble of the steam engine. We were near the railroad crossing just off the end of the trestle.

"Quick, Millie, get two more rocks. Big ones!"

We heard the "toot-toot" of the whistle before we saw the train. Then the big black engine roared around the curve in the trestle, and as it slowed for the crossing, great billows of steam swirled in front like a dragon snorting in anger. Instantly we leaped down the bank to crouch in the salmonberry bushes, our hearts going lickety-split.

The train passed the crossing when it suddenly shuddered, lurched off the tracks with a piercing screech of brakes and came to a jerky stop with blasts of steam boiling into the sky.

All the passengers and crew poured off the train shouting and yelling. Such a babble!

There was much terror in our young hearts. We crawled away out of sight until we hit the park trail, then scrabbled down the bank to the rocky beach. We huddled among the logs wondering if we'd hurt or killed anyone. We did not know what to do. But as dusk fell, hunger and fright drove us home to our houses.

Much later the police arrived at our homes. I was sent to bed with supper. Jimmy was sent to bed with a licking and no supper.

I never knew how my parents coped with the law or whether there was any retribution. I do remember my mother calling me "incorrigible."

Orysia Dawydiak
PIG TALES

As a female graduate student studying animal science, I've had my share of beastly experiences. One of the first occurred when I was sent out to feed six sows in a pasture.

I did not pay attention to their whereabouts as I filled their trough with feed. That was a mistake. I heard some thunder coming from behind, a head appeared between my legs and suddenly I found myself piggyback en route to the trough. Never, never stand between a sow and her chow.

Then came my introduction to breeding procedures. On one occasion, during some very hot and humid weather, I was marking the girls who were "in heat" with a red crayon. I had to stoop to chase a few from a shed and managed to lose the marker from my pocket. I was hot, tired and frustrated. My good humour had melted in the heat. Then one of the gals came out of the shed smacking her painted red lips, looking content. Miss Piggy had found the crayon.

The best ever had to be my lessons on collecting semen from a boar. My supervisor, Duane, was standing outside the pen where I was working with a 600-pound pig. In order to collect the semen, I had enticed the boar to mount a "dummy sow," which was a padded bench bolted to a concrete floor. I danced around him and doubled over, trying to grasp the sheath of his penis without being trampled. I finally had a hold, and tried to manoeuvre a jar into place to collect the semen. The boar was moaning and grunting, so I knew the payload was on its way. Then my hand slipped ever so little. I heard a spluttering behind me. When I looked around, Duane was spitting vehemently and wiping his mouth. It was a hit! I was not.

This pig thing was not for me. Although I graduated with a degree in swine reproductive physiology, I decided to raise sheep instead.

Paulette C. Dilks

HOW WE HAPPENED TO BUY OUR HOUSE AND . . .

So I drove off without saying when I'd be back. We were at that point—either one of us would leave or we'd have to talk. About the future. While I was gone, David bought an old dilapidated house! Well, he hadn't signed the papers yet but he was taken by it. He showed it to me and it got me too.

What we saw as we stood in the big front yard: lilacs, tall Douglas firs and shady maples. An invitation to stay and work things out.

What we could have seen: the puddle of water in the kitchen, original 1912 wiring and plumbing, crumbling chimneys and carpenter ants.

We also did not see The Old Woman. I've never seen her, although a three-year-old house guest solemnly told us she wasn't lonely one night because "the nice old lady stayed with me and read me a story." I figure The Old Woman shooed us past the puddle and waved her hands whenever David or I might have gotten realistic. She liked us. We'd all get along just fine.

I'm not surprised any more when we repaint a room and remove old trim and discover that the new paint *exactly* matches the original colour. Or when I plant yellow freesias and two days later some bloom in the garden. To repaper the living room we removed some door moldings, revealing the old wallpaper, and— you guessed it—we had chosen a nearly identical pattern.

Curiously, I feel good about her help with the decorating and even the occasional friendly visit. The night I was in labour with my firstborn I sat and rocked and almost heard her say, "Don't get so excited—go back to bed. You've got a long time yet!" Well, I *was* excited; I didn't sleep, and two days later when I had my son I was tired. Nobody tells me what to do. Or maybe she does but I don't have to take her advice.

Was it an accident that we found the house and became a family? It sure didn't seem likely the afternoon I drove away. Anyway, now Our Old Woman has a good dog. He died after years of faithful service and we buried him near the walnut tree where he used to watch our kids play. Maybe he still does.

Chris Dunning
OUT OF SERVICE

"Well lads," said Sid, putting his pint of beer down, "we can't hold a candle to them Canadians. Especially their bus drivers.

"It were like this see. Me and Edna were visiting Ted and Helen in Canada. Mississauga, west of Toronto.

"Helen had rented a wheelchair from Red Cross for Edna. Her bad legs you know. Having some time to kill at end of stay, I thought I'd return the wheelchair on my own like.

"It were right hot day as I wheeled the folded chair down to the bus stop. I don't drive and Ted had gone to work.

"I had a few minutes to wait so I unfolded the chair and sat on it. Don't laugh. It were like a furnace out there.

"Anyway along comes the bus. But before I can get up, out jumps the driver and helps me on. Like I was some doddery old gent. All right Fred, no comments!

"Then back he goes again and fetches the chair. All so fast I hadn't time to tell him I could manage on me own. By then see, it was too late. Everyone thought I was an invalid.

"When we reached the terminus, I waited until everyone had got off. Then I asks driver which bus to take for Red Cross like.

"'Don't worry,' says he, winding his sign to show

'Out of Service'. Then off he takes down the road just like a taxi. All the way to the Red Cross. There he takes the chair out of the bus, unfolds it and sits me in it. 'Thank you,' says I and off he goes.

"I tell you Olivier couldn't have done a finer job of impersonating a decrepit old man. Eh, what's that Bert? I don't need to act? Come on! You see I hadn't the heart to hurt that driver's feelings. Let him think he's Florence Nightingale I say.

"Anyroad I sat and waited a few moments before taking the chair into the office. Wouldn't do for the driver to see me now, would it! I can tell you, back at the terminus I hid behind a bus shelter and peered into every bus before climbing on. Just to make sure I didn't get that same driver.

"Did I write the bus company? Well, no I didn't. Could've got him in hot water like. Him leaving his route an' all. No, let sleeping buses lie, says I.

"What's that Harry? Another pint? Eeh, I don't mind if I do!"

BY INVITATION

Timothy Findley
MAKING HISTORY

In 1964, we bought fifty acres of land southeast of Lake Simcoe, Ontario. There was a classic nineteenth-century farmhouse shaded by sugar maples and surrounded by Victorian gardens. The nineteenth-century quality of the gardens—their quietness and loveliness—reminded me of the world depicted in the plays and stories of Anton Chekhov. I couldn't call the place *The Cherry Orchard*,—there were no cherry trees. However, stones abounded—in the fields, along the treelines and in the nearby remains of old barn foundations. Perhaps we should name the place *Stone Orchard*. And that was when the idea occurred to build a stone wall across its front. Thus, when it came time to rent out our land to a neighbouring farm family, part of the deal was a supply of cut fieldstone from the ruined barn foundations on their property.

Soon, a mason was found and the front lawn became littered with piles of stone, chipped clean of their ancient mortar—while a high wall began to rise between the road and the gardens. We heard, around this time, of how one carload of visitors to the neighbourhood had asked their hosts in the nearby village: *who are those idiots south of town, tearing down that lovely old stone wall??*

The whole project took three years to complete—but at last, the day came when the final stone was to be set in place.

It must be celebrated. I had already discovered, while renewing the plaster in one of the rooms, a small parcel tucked away between the studs of one wall. In it were some pages from an 1899 newspaper, and a note telling us who had lived there and what could be seen from the front windows of that time. This message from the past was an inspiration. What form should our time capsule take?

I then got busy with other necessities of the day, so that when the mason was ready to lay the last stone, I panicked. To the tune of his cries of *my mortar is hardening, hurry!* and *it won't wait much longer!* I scurried about, collecting what I thought would be an appropriate container and some significant contents for it: an empty coca-cola bottle and a handful of coins. I hurriedly scrawled a note to the effect that these items— the coke bottle and money—could be seen as the symbols of our age and culture—a time of materialism and not a little triviality. I then added a few phrases about the day's news—it was August, 1971—and signed the note.

As the mason's cries grew more urgent, I stuffed the note into the coke bottle, but most of the coins were too large to pass through its narrow mouth. Undaunted, I grabbed up an empty mayonnaise jar, broke open the coke bottle to retrieve the note, placed note and coins in the mayonnaise jar, screwed on the lid and rushed this hastily made capsule out to the young mason. He dropped it into the waiting cavity, sealed it over with the last of his mortar and fitted the final stone into place. Done.

But, badly done.

It wasn't until the next day that the awful truth dawned on me. Although I had successfully switched the containers, I had not thought to change the note referring to the coca-cola bottle.

And so it is that some future student of old civilizations, sifting through the ruins of an ancient stone wall southeast of Lake Simcoe in Ontario, will come upon the *documented* evidence of a unique sect—the only *wide-mouthed coke culture* in the Western World!

My dithering time capsule may well prove to be an archaeological time bomb.

BY INVITATION

Keath Fraser

"DID THE EARTH NOT SHAKE?"

I think how we handle chance encounters establishes our place in heaven. I'm thinking of the mild earthquake that visited Vancouver in January 1981, just before our last recession. I thought some heavy truck had tipped over in the street. When I saw Georgia Street wave gently like an asphalt ribbon, I did what came naturally to me: cowered in my own arms. When a pane of glass fell from the Scotia tower, as if the building had exhaled its oxygen, I placed my hands on my head. Was I going to hyperventilate?

The shaking lasted ten seconds, no more than fifteen. The Birks' clock on the corner lurched on its pedestal. None of us knew what to make of the city's sudden grogginess, a women in smart clothes clobbered by a mugger. Shopping bags dropped, scarves dangled, overcoats slid down kneecapped bodies. Nothing seemed quite as secure to us now as the past. I took in the present clutching a bus stop pole: traffic lights bouncing on overhead cables: the jammed green signal blinking, blinking: the thick noon traffic coming to a dead stall. A very thin crack, running twelve or fifteen feet, had opened along a curb.

The stillness following was like one minute of silence for those lost in a recent war. I haven't heard such urban silence since. We discovered ourselves in foolish postures, over-balanced in compensation, still fearful for our safety. We must have looked rigid with expectation, awaiting the resumption of artillery shelling from an advance unit of East End guerrillas; or else positioned like dance partners when the music is killed to spotlight the funniest poses. Is exaggeration a natural response to fear? A woman in red flatties had stepped right out of them on the freezing sidewalk.

The bright sun seemed unreal now, and we began finding our shoes, putting overcoats back on. Drivers emerged from cars to rearrange their seatbelts. Everyone resembled lunchtime adulterers preparing themselves for an imminent return to the real world. To respectability, I think. Nobody quite knew whether to stay on for a chat, light up a post-coital weed, or get the hell back to the office pretending nothing juicy had happened. Nobody, except for one man dressed in a stained raincoat and worn-out Hush Puppies.

This crank on the Bay corner, who can still be seen waving his rosary over a framed portrait of Our Crucified Saviour, had recovered rather sooner than most and was now strolling up and down the sidewalk holding his beads aloft and saying calmly—as though he'd told us so a hundred times before (and he probably had)—"What was it Christ said? Do you recall what Our Lord said?" I couldn't remember what Our Lord said, about lubricity or any other cataclysm, but for the moment found myself wishing I did. "Jerusalem," he was reminding us. "Did the earth not shake under Jerusalem?" It was unquestionably this patient man's finest hour.

Jane French

NO AUTOGRAPHS, PLEASE

The South Indian village was straight from an R. K. Narayan novel. The movie being filmed there, *Mysteries of the Dark Jungle*, was inspired by a nineteenth-century Indian adventure book written by an Italian. The set was more Indian than India itself. No cliché from the British raj had been overlooked. Turbaned snake charmers, *beedi*-smoking yogis on beds of nails and mustachioed mahouts atop elephants crowded the marketplace. The multinational crew, adjusting cables and lights while yelling into walkie-talkies in Italian, English, Tamil and Hindi, only added to the chaos.

Indians love crowds, spectacle *and* movies. Hundreds of rapt spectators perched on surrounding rooftops. The day "Hollywood" came to Nanjangud will not be soon forgotten.

As an extra, I played an English lady who curtsied whenever American star Stacy Keach (the Governor) and Italian co-star Virna Lisi (his wife) passed in a horse-drawn carriage. By midday my heat-induced fantasies had Kabir Bedi, the dashing Indian star playing the Maharajah, abducting me from the oven-like bazaar to his secluded palace.

Instead, during a break, I retreated to the shade of a flower vendor's stall. Villagers descended immediately. Since early morning I had been in a Victorian-style wool dress, petticoats and corset. Children touched my costume, women stared at my blond hair and men earnestly inquired about my film career.

It was impossible to convince them I was not a movie star. My efforts were doubly confounded by their limited English. One man pushed a crumpled piece of paper and a pen into my hands, desperate for an autograph. Another grabbed the pen, imploring me to sign the palm of his hand. It was easier to oblige than refuse.

Word spread about the famous foreign movie star. People pushed forward. Again I protested, "I'm only an extra!" The response was a garland of jasmine flowers around my neck. In a nation where stars are worshipped as gods, my fans offered me their devotion. This was an auspicious occasion but I wanted to be alone, an alien concept for Indians.

Famous stars have bodyguards. Mine appeared unexpectedly—policemen wielding bamboo canes pushed the crowd behind rope barriers. My debut as a movie star had ended as abruptly as it began. The only souvenirs were a signature on an unwashed palm and the scent of jasmine.

Janice Garden-Macdonald
WHEN I WAS TEN...

When I was ten, everything was a mystery to me. Life and death. Electricity. And simpler things too—like how a lazy, one-eyed cat was able to catch and swallow Joey. And if he was so smart, why did he leave those tell-tale feathers all over Anne's kitchen? The bird (and the cat) belonged to my next-door neighbour and best friend. So, naturally, when she suggested we have a seance in my basement to bring back the beloved budgie, I agreed.

We descended the stairs cautiously, three girls, taunting the unknown. "If you want this to work, it's gotta be dark." Anne spoke with authority, for she was the oldest.

I turned off the light—a single bulb that dangled above our old chrome table. We were swallowed by the blackness. "Join hands," Anne instructed. We did so, gladly. Her faceless voice became eerie in the pitch dark—my niece tightened her bony grip around my fingers. Anne began to chant a deep alto drone. "Joey . . . Speak to us, great bird-spirit." We were fraught with expectation. "Joey, oh Joey. *E-e-e!*" Suddenly, a chilling shriek! We broke apart, reaching and grasping in the so-thick air, searching for the swinging light chain. My niece, bound to her chair, sat pale and trembling.

"Did you see it?" she screamed. "Did you hear that awful flapping noise?" We pushed and grovelled up the stairway, three abreast. Breathless and gasping, we swore each other to secrecy.

Now, when I think about our basement, I remember mostly the windows, painted shut, and the cold concrete floor. And of course I remember my mother (who had never heard of Margaret Laurence), standing at the top of the stairs screeching in nervous excitement, "Bird in the house!" It wasn't a budgie, but a terrified blackbird who had answered our invitation. My parents never understood how it got in. No open windows, no fireplace flue.

But the explanation was simple enough for three girls—an incarnate budgie, born in the dark basement of a child's wish. And now that I am well away from being ten years old, I am resolute to find—that everything is a mystery to me.

Elizabeth Gourlay

A SONG, A LAY, A LITTLE POEM

Such a strange awakening. Words clamoring against the walls of my mind, pulling me from sleep, words determined to be given utterance. Not words of my own devising, but those of an ancient ditty, learned long ago in childhood.

Three o'clock and I am sitting up in bed reciting:

> A poor old slave has gone to rest,
> I know his bones are free,
> His bones they lie
> Disturb them not
> Way down in Tennessee.

I chant this version, also the one we intoned while skipping rope, in childish pig Latin, "A pickety poor old slickety slave . . . ''

Then the spell, or whatever it was, was broken. Fortunately I soon slept again as the next day was to be busy.

Sophia, young friend and fellow poet, had made arrangements for me to read at the college where she teaches. Despite our age discrepancy, I feel very close to Sophia. Last year her own mother died in particularly tragic circumstances. Sophia is still convalescent in her grief.

The college lies outside the city. Since I own this disability, no sense of direction, Sophia has promised to drive. Perhaps if one faculty is missing, some other is more highly developed.

The reading appears to go well. The room is packed with students, they are attentive, laughing in the proper places, suitably solemn in others. Nowadays, it makes me happy to communicate my vision of the world. During the reading I remark the presence of Sophia, noting her dark, close-cropped head, her heavily fringed brown eyes.

At the conclusion of the reading, I do an extraordinary thing. I find myself recounting to the students the night's strange occurrence, and once again I chant the ancient ditty, giving them both versions. It seems they have never heard the verse before.

I am embarrassed. What on earth will Sophia think? As soon as she returns to the office where I await, I start to apologize.

Sophia smiles, puts her hand gently over my lips.

"Listen," she says.

Then, in a low sweet voice, she sings the same primitive verse.

"You know it?" I ask, astonished.

"Yes, always. Mother sang it to us as a bedtime song ever since I can remember."

Sophia lifts her gaze to mine.

"You relayed her message. To say she is at peace."

After a pause, she adds, "In death one's bones are free."

Shirley Grant

A MAN'S WORD IS HIS BOND (BUT NOT ALWAYS)

Some time ago I was in the isolation unit of a hospital for several months. This might have been lonely, but fortunately I am a radio amateur (a "ham" with call sign VE3BRE) and the hospital administrator was quite familiar with the hobby. Consequently I was allowed to have a small low-power transmitter/receiver in my room.

One night about 2:00 a.m. I was waiting first patiently, then impatiently for the night nurse to take away the bedpan. In desperation I decided to try to lower it to the floor myself, despite having both my right arm and my right leg in a cast. The bed rails were up, but I thought that by leaning over the side far enough, I could carefully lower it to the floor. So I tried out my plan. But with a sudden clank that brought the night nurse running, the rails gave way and slid into the Down position. I tumbled out of bed and into the bedpan!

Some time later, when my heart had stopped thumping and I was back in bed in a clean dry nightgown and with a cup of tea to soothe my jangled nerves, I began to see the funny side of the whole episode. In fact, it seemed so funny that I wanted to share it with someone, so I turned on my ham radio to see if anyone was still up and listening. After calling in on all the frequencies, I finally made contact with another ham. Knowing there was no one else on the air, I recounted my adventure, putting my trust in his promise that he wouldn't tell another soul. After a five-minute conversation and a lot of laughs, I turned off the rig and went to sleep.

Next morning I turned on my ham radio and to my horror and utter dismay, on every frequency I heard other hams roaring with laughter at the story of VE3BRE falling into her bedpan. No matter where I turned the dial, the story was being told over and over again, and to this day I haven't lived it down.

Do you wonder that I no longer put my faith in a man's word?

BY INVITATION

Phyllis Grosskurth
LION TAMING

In October 1980, I published a review-article in the *Times Literary Supplement* on the last volume of Virginia Woolf's letters. The piece caused shock waves because I suggested the possibility that Leonard Woolf might have colluded in his wife's death.

As a result I was inundated by indignant letters from Bloomsburyites. Surprisingly, I received an angry missive from the Shakespearean scholar, A. L. Rowse (no lover of Bloomsbury). He lectured me severely and advised me to listen to my "elders and Betters."

My husband, who has a wicked sense of humour, at dinner one night suggested that we send Rowse a photocopy of his letter with one of my own complaining plaintively that someone else had obviously written the letter and had signed his name. Our guest, a noted art historian, volunteered to write the letter. It was a masterpiece. I apologized to Rowse for bothering him with a minor, embarrassing matter but felt that he should know that some malicious person had sent me the enclosed "hysterical and ungrammatical" letter. I felt that I should inform him of this before I sought legal advice.

The result? For the next six weeks I was inundated with books by A. L. Rowse, all containing flowery inscriptions to me. I must have the largest collection of books by A. L. Rowse outside his personal library.

BY INVITATION

Valerie Haig-Brown
THE DAY EVERYTHING HAPPENED

And then there was the day John and I set out to get the wood. A November chore which we had started the day before. Several inches of snow had already fallen and more was on the way. The big green pick-up was parked on the lawn next to the woodpile where he had left it after unloading the night before. But the door was ajar and the interior light had drained the remaining juice out of the battery. No matter. Just bring the little station wagon down the hill on to the lawn and jump-start the truck.

We were soon bouncing our way out to the far reaches of the ranch where we were cleaning up fallen dead trees along a fence line. A couple of miles over a rough track and through a small slough or two. We only got a little bit stuck on the first route we tried and the morning was only half gone by the time we reached the cutting place. A couple of hours and the truck was loaded as full as we could get it for the return trip. But one rear tire looking kind of soft. Still, we could probably get home on it.

Half a mile along we checked the tire again, just at the bottom of a particularly steep section of track. Very flat. And we already knew that the spare tire was kaput— also flat. Time to abandon truck and walk home—besides, it was past lunchtime and problems are so much easier to face on a full belly.

Bread, cheese and tea; and then drive twenty-five miles to town and get the spare repaired. But the car was stuck on the lawn. Just enough snow so that the hill was too slippery. No problem—brother Charlie only lives a mile away and, even though he is not around, his bigger green pick-up can pull the car out to the road. Didn't take too long and in a couple of hours John had the tire ready. (The only slightly annoying part was that the tire turned out to need nothing but air and we could have got that at Charlie's because he has a compressor in his shop.)

It was late by the time we headed out in Charlie's truck. Snow was beginning to fall, but nothing serious yet. We ground along the track in four-wheel-drive and, leaving Charlie's truck at the top of the steep incline, we rolled the firm tire down to our truck.

But first we would have to lighten the load so we could jack up the truck. About half the load should do it. The ground under the flattened tire was only a little icy. So it wasn't surprising that the jack slipped out the first time. Better lighten the load a little more.

It only took three or four attempts to get the truck jacked up, but by this time there was very little wood left on the truck, and it was really quite dark. With the help of a rapidly fading flashlight the tire was changed and we were ready to roll. All we had to do was chuck the wood back on the truck, and, since there was more snow now and the slope was getting slippery, wisdom dictated that we put half the wood on each truck.

A mere half hour or so later, after backing the other truck gingerly down the slope and pitching half a cord of wood back up off the ground, a two-green-truck procession wended its way slowly through the trees and over the hills and dips and sloughs—without mishap—

all the way back to the woodpile. Unload in the dark and get those trucks "outta here" and back to the road before they get snowed in!

Just another average day on a ranch in the bush on the edge of the Rockies.

Leslie-Ann Hales
THE POTATO, THE BEETLE AND TENPENCE

Glasgow. 1976. Bus strike. Downpour. Me: snuggled up with a cup of tea by my gas fire, quietly enjoying the peaceful gloom of my Victorian basement flat.

Enter Kathy. Good friend, but trouble stalks her, or rather me when I'm around her. First her phone call:

"Leslie-Ann, I'm desperate! I have to be at Central Station for the train to London then the flight to Botswana; not a cab anywhere. Bloody strike. I'm going to have to drive the beetle to the station. This is where you come in."

Sinking Heart. Sly at making plans, Kathy's have a habit of going awry the minute I "come in."

"You drive with me to the station. We'll park, I'll get my ticket, then you just call someone to collect you and the beetle."

I don't have a driver's licence and I wouldn't drive the beetle if I did—no windshield wipers, insurance or road tax. But, as usual, I sighed, agreeing to wade into what I knew wasn't going to work out as neatly as Kathy had constructed.

En route wasn't all that nerve-wracking, except for

the rain and the parade of cabs on the road. At Central, Kathy promptly parked, blocking a huge red sign: NO PARKING. Ordering me to guard the car should a policeman appear (depending on my charming Canadian accent to prevent a ticket), Kathy dashed off to buy her ticket while I waited, precariously balancing a pile of straw hats, appropriate in Botswana, but not in damp, dark, polluted Central Station. Back she ran.

"Now you get in line for me and I'll just leave a note on the windscreen saying you'll only be here a few minutes."

Obediently wandering off, I rather wished I was boarding the London train than dealing with a sick, illegally parked beetle. Moments later, Kathy guiltily reappeared.

"Now, don't panic, Leslie, just a wee accident. Somebody backed into my car; there's bits of it lying around on the pavement. Police want me to press charges, but without insurance, I'm not sure that's a good idea." Heavy sigh. "The train's leaving. Love you! Don't worry. Bye!"

Thank God for lots of ten-Ps in my pocket. Six calls, four hours later, I find two friends reluctantly agreeing to come and rescue the beetle . . . and me. I explain that the potato on the dashboard is to rub over the windshield; keeps the rain off, sort of. Two miles from Central to my flat; Kathy reached London before I got home. One tenpence left. Enough for a fire.

BY INVITATION

David Helwig

NIGHT WORK ON THE DAYLINER

I don't think I'll mention the name of my partner in crime. He does have a criminal record. Still, it was a long time ago.

A conference in Kingston, and I was there representing the TV drama department of the CBC. My home was in Kingston, but I worked five days a week in Toronto. After the first day of the conference I invited some people round to my house. The evening passed, and we drank a good deal of Scotch. At two or three in the morning I set out to drive the last guest to his hotel. Though he had a criminal past, he now had a new career and a respectable wife, and by the time we reached the hotel, he decided that he was lonely for her and wanted to set off home.

I drove him to the station to get the middle-of-the-night train. And though I commuted by train every week, I managed to forget that the Kingston station had relocated a few months before. So we drove to the old station. And there, sure enough, was a train. The station itself was locked, but on the track beside it was a two-car dayliner, with the lights on and the engine running.

So we got on. The train was empty, though the trainmen had left some of their things in one of the seats.

An empty train, the engine running, the lights on and not a soul aboard at three in the morning. My passenger found this too ghostly altogether and decided he wanted to be taken to the highway, where he'd hitchhike to Toronto.

"Wait a minute," he said, as we were getting back in the car. "Want a hat?"

I'm not sure what I said, but back he went to the train. When he returned he threw something in the back seat and off he went to the highway.

In the morning I woke, sick and hung over, got the kids off to school, and only then remembered that I had something illicit in my car. I went in and looked.

Two hats, two coats, keys, notebooks and presumably everything the trainmen had needed to run the train at 7 a.m. that day.

What to do?

Could I take it all out in the country and dump it? No.

So what to do?

Later that morning, a large anonymous parcel was mailed in Kingston, addressed to the local station. The next time I got on the dayliner, as I did once a week, I noticed that the trainmen had begun locking their coats overnight in the office of the new station.

I didn't tell this story for several years.

The dayliner doesn't run any more.

Winifred N. Hulbert
USED NEEDLE

Aged September's golden Saturday: a great day to be alive! I was home on the farm for the weekend—home from

Minnedosa, Manitoba, where Grade Twelve schooling kept me all week.

In the early afternoon, teaspoon in hand, I informed Mother, "I'm going for honey." Brother Bert was extracting in his bee-house. Mm-m-m . . . clover's sweetness transformed!

Veiled and gloved, Bert was at his hives. Standing back, I watched and waited, silently.

Then, a stab behind my ear. "I'm stung!"

Almost immediately, fingers and toes tingled. I kept swallowing, then thought of the blueing bag. Some force drove me to that reputed remedy; to a drink of cold water; upstairs to Mother's room. Weak-kneed, I sank into her rocker.

"Did you get your honey?"

"No . . . a sting."

Mother's gaze was intent.

"I feel awful. Mother . . . do something . . . quick . . ."

Everything was revolving. She helped me onto her bed, then stood on a chair at the window—open at the top—shouting, "Bert, quick! Help me!"

I sensed his presence and her voice on the telephone, before drifting off. Most of the following I learned later, in bits and pieces, from those concerned.

Our Dr. Bowman was not home. "Central" located him. He phoned Mother assurance.

Meantime, Mother's best friend, an RN, and daughters Florence (my best friend) and Caroline were in their raspberry patch beyond reach of telephones. Caroline went to the house for a drink—the phone rang. Word of colourless lips brought nurse's advice: a mustard plaster on my heart.

Mother remembered some already bought, ready-made mustard plasters in her bedroom cupboard. Water from her bedroom jug—and a plaster was in place.

Bert was racing our Whippet the two miles and back, fetching Mrs. Wilmot.

She found no pulse and a barely perceptible heart-beat. (Bee's venom, injected into a vein, goes straight to the heart, a rare hazard.) Under woollen blankets, I dreamed of people massaging my legs and arms.

As he lifted my head, Dr. Bowman's voice buzzed, "Swallow this." I obeyed, and vomited.

Unknown to me, my bowels moved. Again, the buzzing. "Best thing that could have happened!"

After that, black silence.

Weeks later, Florence confided, "That day—you, unconscious for five hours—it really made me think."

Me too. Ever since, I've pondered the purpose behind "happenings." That day—through perfect timing—the frayed ends of my life-thread were spliced by the Master Hand.

And I learned an invaluable truth.

Bonnie Koe
BAGGING THE FOOD

My husband, my son and I managed to keep up fairly competently as we handled the cooking in our restaurant one particularly busy after-fiveish supper hour. My daughter worked most of the tables to avoid mixups, because the young woman helping on the front happened to be an employee that we accepted when Manpower Canada asked us if we would hire her through their special program, with the understanding that they would reimburse us for half the wages paid in the first three months. A total lack of experience resulted in easy confusion and so one of us usually monitored her movements quite closely in order to avoid situations that we wouldn't be able to easily rectify.

On this eve, my husband knew that my daughter had her hands full without worrying about the trainee's tables, and at the first sign of anxiety on the trainee's part, he suggested that after her customers took their leave, she could help by handling incoming phone calls. We were all close by to help if questions arose. At this point, she was nearing the last few weeks of the training phases as programmed by Manpower, and the average phone-in orders are simply a statement of menu choices, pick-up times, or delivery addresses, and the phone number for us to call back in case we experience stock depletions. Our little lady hung one order on the rack which totalled just under three hundred dollars and it contained quite a variety of items, so we were relieved to note that the pick-up time allowed us three hours. At 8:30 p.m. we were bagging the food, and she came over and stood nearby watching us. I thought she was interested because she had never observed us preparing an order that large to pack up. What she said, though, as we stapled the bill to one of the bags, is a much better joke now than we could appreciate at the time.

She said, "They wanted that for eight p.m. tomorrow night!"

Lois Kurtz
MIRACLE IN HONG KONG

For months we'd been planning our trip back to Canada and the eventful day had finally arrived. John and I, with our friend Joe, who was helping with the luggage, left for the airport in a Hong Kong downpour.

The rain was falling in torrents when our taxi driver pulled into the queue at the departure level of Kai Tak Airport. As we jumped out, the Cantonese driver seemed to indicate that he would pull ahead under the overhang so we could remove the luggage without getting soaked. Imagine our horror when he not only pulled ahead but slowly drove off with our three suitcases and carry-on bag containing money, passports and airline tickets.

Joe, reacting quickly, ran down the road after the cab with arms flailing and was soon lost from view in that crowd of taxis, umbrellas and people. John had the presence of mind to memorize the licence number of our runaway taxi and took off in search of the police. I stood in a daze on the sidewalk. "God, this can't be happening to us but if it is, please bring that taxi back."

John returned saying the police were alerted to find the missing taxi. That could take hours, and by that time we had only one left to catch our plane. Thinking the driver might have gone to the arrivals area in search of another fare, John went in that direction.

But where was Joe? He'd jumped into another cab with the words, "Follow that taxi." And like something out of a movie the chase began. When the road divided Joe said, "Turn left," although he'd already lost sight of our runaway driver. Soon two lanes of traffic became four and there were dozens of identical red taxis on the road. Joe suddenly shouted, "That's him!" And when the suspect taxi stopped for a traffic light he apprehended it. Our bags were still there and the driver's explanation in Cantonese all the way back to the airport seemed to indicate that he wasn't a thief, only regretful.

I was still standing stunned at the departures entrance when the miracle happened. Suddenly Joe was grinning at me through the rain-streaked windows of a cab and I knew we were going to catch our flight after all.

Christopher Lambie

SLEEPING LOUD

I worked one summer as a tree planter in Northern Ontario. Half an hour after my final exam, my girlfriend had me packed into a stuffy overnight train with a tent, my sleeping bag, a bottle of cheap wine and a used copy of Byron's collected works.

Our camp was in an old abandoned quarry. The tents were pitched around the rim of the site and the cook shack was centred in the gravel pit below us. Every night, after a long day's battle with the heat, insects and thousands of seedling trees, we would climb the banks to our canvas oasis and pass out with the sun in the dirty clothes we planted in all day.

While my tent was usually soaked with rain, pitched on rocks and crowded with gear, the comfort of sleep I found under its sheltering folds seemed a rich luxury. When my alarm sounded in the morning frost, it was an extreme effort to stretch my stiff arm out into the cold dark and turn off the intruding noise.

One night, after nearly two months of this routine, the camp sprang to wakefulness in the 3 a.m. darkness. A huge black bear had broken into the food storage tent and was brawling noisily with the cook's dog.

The crew boss scared him off with a warning shotgun blast, but nobody got much sleep after that. All night, calls travelled from tent to tent as the paranoid fear of being woken by a bear became a pervasive factor in the evening.

The next afternoon we returned to camp, more tired than ever, to be greeted by a horrible sight. The bear had ripped a six-foot gash in one girl's tent just to eat a bottle of skin cream. Obviously the lotion had smelled too sweet to resist. All soaps, deodorants and bug repellents were quickly disposed of in the garbage pile. Nobody wanted the bear as a tent-mate.

After dinner everyone was issued a large pot and a spoon with instructions to bang and make a racket should the bear turn up again that night. I was a little skeptical about this one, but I took my pot and headed off to bed.

Not three hours later, a noise outside my tent prompted me to start banging and shouting like a madman. Soon the whole camp kicked in with a chorus of fear-laden cacophony and the three camp dogs proceeded to run wildly around the rim of the quarry, looking for the bear.

After thinking about it for a few minutes, I calmly undid the zipper of my tent to find a fat raccoon playing three feet away from my door. Instead of informing the others that it was only this little pest, however, I crawled back into my cozy nest and fell back to sleep with the echoes of dozens of pots clanging in my ears and the dreams of how many more hundreds of trees I would be able to plant than anyone else the next day.

BY INVITATION

Dorothy Livesay

WORD OF MOUTH

Recently I have been most interested in collecting anecdotes from elderly people who are often in a sorry plight. Indeed, what happened to me along this line occurred only a few months ago.

Like most seniors, I have dentures. One is for comfort and the other for good looks.

One day recently I was cleaning up my tiny bathroom and washing my dentures in the basin. I laid them on the edge of the sink and they slipped into the toilet bowl just I was flushing it. My left arm plunged in after, but the teeth slipped right out of my hand farther down the drain in the onrush of water.

A young plumber was consulted, who said that a search for my denture could only take place in the summer.

A week later, due to major flooding in the house, the landlady called the plumber again. Now her water pipes were blocked. He dug and dug and found that one of the circular blades used for pumping water into the house had got entangled with one black sock (not mine). It was then retrieved and the hole covered up. The plumber repeated his admonition that a search for my denture could take place only during the summer months.

Disappointed, I returned to my room, but was soon called out into the front garden. The plumber was walking toward me, smiling, holding out a large spade. "Look," he said, "would this be yours?"

There on the spade was my denture, turned black and mucky but still entirely whole.

Back in the kitchen I plunged my teeth into boiling water, scrubbed them with Javex, and carried them triumphantly into the dining room to exhibit my trophy to my fellow boarders. One of them gasped: "Surely, you're not going to WEAR them!"

"Why not?" I said, and popped them into my mouth.

Carolyn Luke
TERRIBLE TRUTH

Do you have beautiful and big brown eyes?
Then a word of caution I would advise
for the tale I impart is wholly the truth
and occurred one day to my lovely Aunt Ruth.

She but rubbed her finger upon a closed eyelid
and her beautiful eye plopped out of her head
and just like a whack-o ball on elastic thread
it quivered and shimmied and slithered and slid.

As fast as she could, Ruth rushed into the house
where lounged Uncle Gerry, her long-time spouse,
who medically no longer was allowed to drive—
but took over the wheel in a wild, country-road ride.

Cupping her eye in a tissue, Ruth sadly did moan,
"I do hope they can fix it, for it's the best eye I own."
"A most rare occurrence," the doctor did declare,
as he popped it back in with much savoir-faire.

So should your eyes itch, remember Aunt Ruth,
who found out for herself this terrible truth—
you must treat itchy eyes with the utmost care
for an eyeball hanging out is a living nightmare.

J. L. McClennan
THE ABLUTION BLOCK

Time spent working in one of the remotest parts of Australia provided me with numerous unique experiences, of which the following anecdote is but one example.

Poisonous snakes are by far the most dangerous aspect of land-based, Australian wildlife. This fact became emblazoned on my memory when I first stepped into our construction site office, for one wall of the office was covered with a cheerful display of the more common deadly snakes indigenous to Australia. The colourful chart was there so you could chase down the offending reptile after it bit you, and identify it, so that the medical team rushing to your assistance could determine what antivenin to use. Just how this was to be accomplished, considering we were hours away from any such assistance and many snakes' bites produced fatalities within half an hour, totally escaped me! Nor was I reassured when I enquired about antivenins, as I was informed that no one carried antivenin, since only a few dozen people died from snake bite annually.

As a Canadian not used to deadly snakes, I spent my walkabouts thereafter with my eyes fastened to the ground. Having mastered the technique, I was somewhat chagrined to discover that there were also an untold number of large tree pythons hovering about. But that is another story.

The ablution block was a biffy with a makeshift flushing mechanism that we had set up near the office. Since it contained water, small frogs often made their way into it, any water in that very dry part of Australia being very attractive to wildlife. The occasional impact of the cheeky, frolicking frogs was a startling disruption to one's reverie that we came to accept.

One afternoon I was in the office when a co-worker came tearing in yelling, "snake in the ablution block!" Not only was it in the shack, but it had followed the appetizing frogs into their porcelain pond, and was discovered curled around underneath the seat cover. At this announcement, all the Australians raced out to teach the snake a lesson, except for our secretary, who turned white, as she had just returned from the ablution block a few minutes before!

After the ablution block had been practically destroyed catching the snake, we had coffee and joked about sucking out poison, and who might have discovered whom was a true friend, and we all lived nervously thereafter!

BY INVITATION

George McWhirter

WATER RING

The ring I bought for getting married was at a discount from a friend. He was someone we now call physically disadvantaged, who needed a wheelchair and had a small hump. He owned a jewellers in Kilkeel.

That June, when my wife and I went swimming at Millisle, the ring dropped away into the kelp.

What did it signify? Was the marriage sunk already? I used to swim a lot in the Irish Sea. Was the water jealous, wanting something to show for all the time I'd spent in it? Or (perish the idea) did the sea want me wedded to the weeds?

I quit the pathetic fallacies and heeded the physiology. While I was warm, the ring fit, but dipped in frigid water, my finger shrank and the plain wedding band was forfeit.

I bought a second ring from the same jeweller and this one spent a lot of its time tied into the string of my swimming trunks. On dry land, I would keep finding it in the fingers of my gloves after a cold wait in the cinema queue. Finally, it was put away in a bedside drawer, in a velveteen pouch.

However, I always felt married and prayed for some token to display it. The years passed. We came to Canada, and when we moved into our present house, my wife dug up a ring in the front garden.

I examined it to see if it was the one from Millisle

that had worked its passage to Canada. But it wasn't; it had a bevelled edge and didn't fit. Ten years married, what miracle would give me the right ring, or a finger fat enough to hold it?

Then, would you believe, a ganglion I had in my wrist shifted to my ring finger. The garden-grown ring held, but the ganglion kept swelling until the bevels cut like a circular saw into the webbed skin between the fingers.

I soaped the ring off and, in its place, have been left with a bezel of gristle I twist constantly—the way a normal person would their wedding ring while they brood over the groceries or the mortgage.

"How does it feel to be the owner of an organic ring?" someone said gleefully, "that won't disappear unless you slam it with a hammer?"

I don't know. This love-bond may be a metaphor for the natural order of our marriage, or pure sorcery—a ring of gristle devised for me by my physically challenged friend, the wizard of wit and fit from Kilkeel?

One night after the loss of the first ring, when we were drinking in the Kilmorey Arms, he tapped his back and told me, "I guarantee you, George. She'll be like this mate of mine. Once ye've got her on good, the divil himself won't get her off you."

But decide for yourself what his warranty was for: wife or ring or ganglion.

BY INVITATION

Michael Mercer

PINK ELEPHANTS

An actor friend of mine—I'll call him Stan—lives in Toronto. He has two children, who at the time of this unfortunate event had reached a point in their young lives that his wife termed "that troublesome in-between age." To Stan, this simply meant they were too old for the crib, and too young for prison.

It was, of course, the children that were Stan's immediate source of agony that fateful Sunday morning. He had imbibed alcohol in a suicidal frenzy at a cast party the previous night, and was comatose in bed with a monumental hangover, when one of the little angels levered his eyelid open and pointed out that he had promised to take them to the wildlife safari park that day. The morning light shredded his optical nerves, and the youthful high voices tore at his few remaining brain cells like pit bulls. He pleaded, begged, wheedled and whined, but when his wife joined the rising chorus of protests, he surrendered to the inevitable. After several aspirins and a piece of dry toast, he surreptitiously slipped a flask of whisky into his jacket and followed them out to the car with all the animation of a broken robot.

It was one of those scalding, humid Toronto days that provides all the joy of taking a bath in sulfuric acid, and when they finally reached the park, Stan's agonies were intensified when he saw the sign warning visitors to keep their windows shut. It was one of those preserves where the animals run free and the humans are caged in their cars. After cruising past numerous toothed and clawed creatures and finally reaching an open area where the elephants roamed, the closed car was an oven. The elephants appeared harmless enough to Stan, so he told his children to roll down the rear windows a few inches, and he and his wife did the same in the front. Within moments, three curious elephants crowded in close to the car, and the first warning Stan had of the cataclysm to follow was the screaming in the back.

An elephant had poked his trunk in the rear window, and in terror, one of his children quickly wound it up, closing it on the animal's appendage. Then all hell broke loose. The elephant began trumpeting in pain and kicking at the car; Stan was shouting at the screaming children to open the window, and his wife was just screaming. Then the two other elephants came to aid their companion and flailed their huge feet repeatedly into the rear of the car, rocking it about and smashing out the tail-lights. Somehow Stan managed to struggle over the seats, wind down the window to free the elephant's trunk, clamber back behind the wheel and race away from the raging pachyderms.

Outside the park, he pulled into a picnic area, and they all collapsed in the shade to recover. The rear of the car was hammered in, and Stan was shaking and babbling like an idiot. It was nearly nightfall before he could get behind the wheel again, and only then after taking a long swallow of whisky from his flask.

They were halfway home when the Ontario Provincial Police pulled them over to the side of the road. For Stan it was most definitely the last straw. His head was thumping, his children crying and his wife lecturing him on the foolishness of putting down the windows in the park. He slammed out of the car and walked back to have an open exchange of views with the two officers who were examining the rear of his car. One of them was writing out a ticket for his lack of tail-lights, while the other approached him and gestured at the car.

"How did you get this damage back here?"

Stan wheeled on him and growled, his breath laden with whisky fumes.

"How the hell do you think?! It was kicked in by a bunch of damn elephants!!"

Stan spent the night in jail, had his licence suspended and his wife refused to speak to him for a week. It just wasn't his day.

Catharyn E. Miller

ACCIDENTS DO HAPPEN, OR THE HAT THAT WASN'T

There's an old saying that sometimes you can't see the forest for the trees. Likewise, it is equally true that sometimes an alligator in the woodpile can be mistaken for just another log, a lesson I learned the hard way.

It all began one warm, summer evening when my friends, Eileen and Margie, and I decided to do a little window shopping downtown. It costs nothing to look and being that our wallets were a little thin at the time, it seemed like a good way to kill a few hours. Besides, it might even be FUN and INTERESTING.

Everything was going great until we happened upon

a *very* expensive and *very* exclusive ladies' wear store. Partly out of curiosity about how the other half lives, and mostly just because we were there, we decided to go in. Now, in *this* particular store, "exclusive" and "expensive" seemed to be synonymous with "unusual" and even "bizarre." We pawed through the dresses, looked over the sportswear, then stumbled on to the accessories department. There were hats and belts and purses and scarves and hair clips and stockings and other unidentifiable objects everywhere. Giving the merchandise a quick once-over, we zeroed in on the hats.

The striking feature about these hats was their amazing similarity. All of them resembled old-fashioned bathing caps woven out of nylon straw. All but one, that is. This one exception came with ornamental loops dangling from the sides. Naturally, that was the one we decided to try on first. I put the hat on my head and tried to tie the loops under my chin. They didn't reach. Eileen thought there was something wrong with the loops. Margie thought they were just intended to dangle as decorations. I tended to side with Margie. It was then that the salesgirl decided to enter the discussion. Approaching me, she asked, "Do you know that you're wearing a purse?"

Managing to maintain a poker face, I replied, "So *that's* why the loops didn't tie!" Then, hastily replacing the "hat" on the counter, I followed my friends outside where we broke down in peals of laughter.

BY INVITATION

Mavor Moore
CULTURAL EXCHANGE

In the spring of 1981, while I was chairman of the Canada Council and Charles Lussier its director, we were invited to visit China to discuss cultural exchange. The malefic Gang of Four were gone, and Maureen Forrester and the Toronto Symphony had just had a sensationally successful tour. In the national interest we invited our distinguished wives—mine a singer and his a sociologist—to accompany us at their own expense.

At six o'clock in the morning of our last day in Beijing, after a fruitful but hardly precedent-setting week, Alexandra and I were awakened by a call from the commercial attaché of the Canadian Embassy, a young man name Higginbottom. He had just received a call from the Chinese government; the ambassador was out of town for the weekend; the estimable cultural attaché, Mary Sun, was unreachable, and could he meet us for breakfast as soon as possible. Over eggs benedict at the hotel, we learned that in an hour we were to meet Vice-Premier Bo-Yibo, a veteran economist who had spent some time in Canada. The embassy, it seemed, had been trying to get in to see him all year. Our unexpectedly successful visit had provided the open sesame, and would I please quiz the Vice-Premier about China's five-year economic plan. How the hell could I introduce economics, I asked, in a meeting about culture? Higginbottom, who had the advantage of speaking Chinese, begged me to try.

At the appointed time we appeared in the Great Hall and were ushered into the presence of Bo-Yibo, multiplied by a couple of dozen dignitaries and functionaries. He and I were seated to right and left of a small table, facing the television cameras with our translators and colleagues nearby. He began by saying that cultural exchange was very important. "How important," I asked, "in relation to other kinds of international relations?" "There is *nothing* more important," he said firmly. I agreed for my own part, but allowed that the Canadian government, in the face of economic restraint, was having trouble financing even modest cultural exchanges. "And by the way," I added, "how's your own five-year plan going?"

The translators went pale and Lussier studied the ceiling, but Higginbottom's pen flew to attention. The old economist laughed and allowed that China, too, was having troubles. "It's a matter of priority," he said, reminding me of Confucius. "If we wish to trade with each other, we must first get to know each other. Where are your books, your films, your plays, your music, your art?" Higginbottom was writing furiously.

Unable to answer for the government, I replied that his message would be welcomed by Canada's artists. And after an hour's useful discussion of ways and means, we left. At the airport, I asked Higginbottom if he had any special message for the mandarins in Ottawa. He said, "Tell them cultural exchange comes before trade and commerce, not after. They won't believe me."

They didn't believe me, either.

Barry K. Morris
BROTHER IN NEED

I do not recall the exact date of Martin Luther King Jr.'s death in 1968, but I know where I was...and that I almost was not.

I had been a theological student at the south-side Chicago Theological Seminary, and took my turn living with various members of the extensive, well-organized Blackstone Rangers. Two young Blacks with considerable charisma organized, in turn, many other local leaders to form an impressive network, or "gang of gangs," all in the tenuous process of making a transition from illegal to quasi-political activity.

I held the meek but not so mild job of staying overnight with the Rangers at a Seminary-owned house, and occasionally, driving them to and from court appointments, job interviews, hospitals and sometimes, suddenly—without prior consultation—into enemy turf.

On one occasion, thinking that I was nobly driving a vanful to the County Hospital for visits, we took a directed turn into Devil's Disciples' "cribs" (a term for locally controlled territory, by them or any gang). Rangers disembarked and then, with gunfire noise filling the hot air, tried to jump back into the VW van. We took a barrage of some kind of fire, but somehow I then had the sense to cut out of that area, with doors still open, including the driver's. All were spared and I developed tangible respect for gang battles, even of the mildest kind.

I never could quite drive the same, tame way again. I had not lost too much nerve to continue working with the Rangers, though. The day came, all too soon, when out of a serene blue sky, word broke out and spread as fast as zip gun bullets, that Martin Luther King had been shot dead. Heavy clouds of severe depression, or so I opined, spread heavily and swept low.

I was driving Rangers that day and somehow felt that, as a Seminarian, with some Black students, and . . . with a batch of seemingly "good deeds" under my moral black belt, I would always be protected; at least, in Ranger-controlled territory. No such luck—protection comes, if it does, as both luck and as providence. It happened—

As the afternoon ended, I had been driving one last Ranger, a John L., back to the house. He asked to be let off at the corner drugstore and—I now recall vaguely— he waved me on. I was not sure whether to wait up for him, or not. It was sure hot, and heavy.

Seemingly ordinary numbers of usual hangers-on mushroomed quickly into a strange score of many. Suddenly the van was surrounded. I must have sensed instinctively that conversation, this time, was out! Time stood still—or was it that time rushed so fast that it surpassed ordinary calculations? I saw fear; I felt fear; my bladder passed fear in sudden spurts, not dribbles. I rolled up the window, I sat tight.

The van got rocked and rocked. It got lighter. If it was not going to levitate, it was going to roll over with me in it, an entrapped, perhaps sacrificed victim to the angry gods of that deeply wild, indignant day.

I began to give in, being powerless and a bit— strangely—on their side. I too felt the need for a sacrifice—some stoning action. But me? Now? Here? Without prior consent? Me—a virtually unconditional, always available driver, who rarely questioned his destinations?

"Come sweet death," I thought. (Darn those textbook titles from Older Testament classes!)

With my own smell—of fear—of impending end—

closing, alas, John L. arrived. I had not been expecting him, but he broke through the heavy crowd, who were virtually in a frenzy, whipped into a collective executioner mood. He shooed them forth and away, like the unquestioned Shepherd that he truly was. The crib was his, as he was their servant and leader put through too many tests, battles, night patrols, endless errands, Ranger patronage or broker of goods and services to be challenged now.

Thank God . . . for saviours in the midst of our plain sins and hindsight of what vengeance tries to extract.

Years later I heard—but sadly short of a last visit to say thanks again—John Lett had been killed. I flashed back upon many late night rides in that old VW van, with bullets still lodged somewhere in the rear motor cover. Like times when John would coax me to drive him to pick up his then sweetheart Sandy, as she got off work.

John L: Thanks for being a brother in need, indeed . . .

Leila Nair

PLANCHETTE

The year was 1943. The place, a remote village about 10 km from the west coast town of Tellicherry in South India. Madhavi, a widow, lived in a mud hut on the fringes of a coconut grove that belonged to the landowner she worked for. Her only son had dropped out of school at sixteen and lied about his age to find his way into the Indian Army. Soon after, she started receiving a monthly allowance from her son. But that break was short-lived. it stopped with a killed-in-action notification. It took her another year to become aware of the fact that she qualified for a pension.

That is where my father came in. We lived in "the big house" in the village. My father, then little more than forty years old, was treated something like a village elder. He also handled any correspondence that had to be done in English, for those who sought his help. Madhavi, eventually, did just that.

The reply to Madhavi from the government was that pension benefits would be sanctioned to her—if, and only if, she could furnish the particulars of her son's battalion and serial number. All that Madhavi could say was that her son had been in "the military."

Those were the days of a planchette craze among young adults in India. That age group in our extended family proved no exception, and they managed to find a medium in my ten-year-old sister. My father had shown neither belief nor disbelief in what was going on, but stayed an indulgent bystander to the hilarious communion with the supernatural that rocked our family most evenings. Now, he turned up at a session with an appeal for help on Madhavi's behalf.

A "spirit" identifying itself as Cox, a German, provided the details: the name of the battalion, and the serial number, complete with alphabets and numerals. My father was less than sanguine when he sent them in. But they correctly located Madhavi's son in the army records, and her much-needed pension was on its way.

As a footnote, I must add that my enterprising cousins got after "Cox" to give them the winning number on the Lotto 6/49 of the times—the Calcutta Sweeps. Cox good-humouredly parried them all the way, adding that he broke his code only when it meant unequivocal, rightful benefits to one in need.

BY INVITATION

Toni Onley

SOME OTHER HAND

John Reeves, the Toronto photographer renowned for his portraits of artists and writers, had been commissioned by CP Air's in-flight magazine to do a photo essay about me—"The Flying Artist" or some such thing!

On September 6 we went up to the Bishop Glacier on the shoulder of Mount Garibaldi, but we had got a late start and the weather was poor so we stayed only half an hour. The next day would be better, I promised. Our plan was to go up to the highest glacier in the area, the Cheakamus, at 8,000 feet; to land on it, do some painting and photography; and then go down 1,000 feet to a spectacular glacier on Mamquam Mountain, after which we would return to the Bishop, down at 5,000 feet, so that John could see the peaks of Garibaldi that had been clouded in the first day.

The next morning we got onto the Cheakamus without trouble, but it was not so easy to get off. The winds were gusting—one minute calm, the next up to forty knots, not unusual in the mountains—and the snow was wet and sticky, which slowed the takeoff down the face of the glacier. I waited for the winds to die, then started my first run, but I couldn't get a good speed because of the snow. So halfway down I chopped the power and taxied back up the steep knoll for a second try. My first tracks were packed ice now, so I shouldn't have had another problem with speed. I waited for the winds to drop, then I fired off again, holding in the tracks. When I reached the end of them I had enough speed to take off. I pulled on full flaps, which is usually sufficient to "pop" the plane off the ground by moving the weight from the skis to the wings. But nothing happened. It felt as if I had no flaps, that the wings were flat. I looked out and saw that the flaps were in position. I also saw that the gusting winds had caught up with us. Fine snow was blowing on the surface of the glacier in the direction we were going. That meant my wings had no lift. Essentially, though we were going fifty miles per hour, we were standing still.

It was too late to stop and turn. My options were to chop power, slow, and drop into the horizontal crevasse that stretched ahead, fifty feet wide and two hundred feet deep; or maintain power, try to leap the crevasse, and hope we wouldn't smash into the crevasse's ice wall or slide across the other side and drop into the next wide crevasse that loomed ahead. In retrospect, I made the right decision. I held power and we leaped the first crevasse. Then, by the greatest good fortune, the plane nestled into a narrow, perpendicular crevasse. It was the only one on the mile-wide glacier that ran in the direction of our descent; it formed the stubby stem of a T immediately across from where we jumped the broad crevasse; and it was just wide enough to accommodate the body of the plane while supporting the wings. It minimized the impact of the crash yet prevented us from sliding on toward the next fall. Six feet to the right or left and we would have smashed into the ice.

I would like to say that this was a magnificent piece of flying, but the truth is that I had lost control. Some other hand had pushed us into the only place that could have stopped our fall and cradled us through the long night.

BY INVITATION

P. K. Page

THE SECOND ACCIDENT: GRAÇIAS Ā ZEUS!

I drove the new roller-coaster expressway—on which, if there is a speed limit, few respect it—from the outskirts of Mexico City to the Plaza in its centre. There I parked my *coche* and tipped the boy who offered to guard it in my absence.

On my return some hours later, I exchanged courtesies with the boy and started home, circling the Plaza. The light was green at the first corner, green again at the second. At the third corner the light was red, and I stepped on the brake.

To say "nothing happened" is to misrepresent the whole event, for the car—that once docile and co-operative machine—turned suddenly into a wild animal, and I—from an unhurried, ten-miles-an-hour crawler—became an instant Phaeton driving the horses of the Sun. I shot through the crosswalk at a rate seemingly faster than any driver on the expressway, missing a walking girl by what must have been a hair, heard her terrified screams. I'd have screamed, too, if I hadn't been so busy. Was I reaching for the hand brake? Turning off the ignition? Praying? Rolling agonized eyes to heaven? I have no memory of what I was doing, for the laws of movement, laws I had previously taken for granted, had altered. I was trying to figure them out. Objects whizzed past me at an astonishing rate, whizzed left or right or crabwise on the concrete. Some seemed almost to whiz backwards. And—brake pedal flat to the floor—I whizzed too. Past them, over them, round them, about. Horns blared; tires squealed.

I whizzed on.

And then, miraculously, the second accident occurred. The most perfect accident imaginable. I hit a cab. Its driver a passive, unwitting Zeus to my Phaeton. I read unbelieving fury on his face as I struck him; saw an angry crowd surging round me as I stopped. It was as if all the pedestrians in the Plaza converged upon me instantly, gesticulating, glaring. *Gringa!* they yelled, threatening, enraged. They hated me. But I didn't care. I had stopped. Stopped. The miracle of it! I wanted to kiss the cabbie who had managed to be just there, in exactly the perfect position for me to hit him. Might I not otherwise be travelling still? faster than I ever dreamed of travelling on the freeway—a helpless passenger in a manic machine.

There is more to this story, of course. The girl, the cabbie and I, the wretchedly damaged cars and the plug-ugly Mexican police must all have versions to tell.

Kay Parley
LOGIE BUCHAN KIRK

For as long as I could remember I had dreamed of visiting Scotland and seeing the places my grandmother always talked about so fondly: Cruden Bay, the Nethermill, Ellon, and Logie Buchan Kirk. The kirk, which translates from the Scots as "The Church of Stony Hollow," was where my grandmother's marriage banns were published. It was also the church my grandfather was attending prior to his coming to Canada.

My visit to Scotland was like a pilgrimage, and discovering Logie Buchan was to be one of the highlights. I hired a bicycle at Ellon and strapped my handbag to the handlebar, slung my movie camera over my shoulder, and set off to find the kirk. After half a mile, I found to my consternation that I had no brakes. This was awkward, for although I was off the main highway I could only start down a slope if I could see the end of it, as I never knew where there would be a long winding hill. Usually there wasn't, but I was then left without momentum and trudging up the opposite slope pushing the bike.

I had progressed in this fashion for some time when I entered a farmyard. A small collie dog barked at me but was easily hushed into familiarity. I found it a very comfortable spot, the road winding between the barn and hayricks and the houseyard. A man and wife and two grown-up sons were working in the walled garden, under many tall trees. I stopped the bike and asked the boy nearest the wall for directions. He had a thick Buchan burr, a sun-reddened face, and friendly eyes.

"Aye, that's Logie Buchan Kirk," he nodded, pointing. "Richt roond there."

I thanked him and started off. I could see a building in the distance, beyond the River Ythan, and though it didn't look like a kirk I was sure he had pointed in that direction. There was a long hill, and the road bent, crossed a bridge and eventually wound past my destination. I would have to dismount and walk, or I would never make that turn across the bridge. Then, in one of those moments of stark panic, I realized that there was an optical illusion in the slope and already my bike was rolling out of control. Using what I thought was commendable emergency thinking, I deliberately nosed the bike to the long grass of the ditch, prepared to throw myself clear of the collision when it came. It would be far easier than drowning in the Ythan, and I don't swim.

The tumble was even easier than I had expected. My purse and camera were unscratched. My body was completely unharmed except that I gave my left wrist such a wallop on the handlebar that I succeeded in breaking a ganglion I had been trying to get rid of for six months.

"It's a miracle," I said to myself, as I sat in the grass and stared at the flattened wrist where the unwanted swelling used to be.

Then I looked up and found myself in front of a stone building which had been hidden behind the farmer's trees. I was sitting at the gate of Logie Buchan Kirk.

Steven Pendretti
CALM BEFORE THE STORM

The combination of boat, bus and plane had made a long day of the trip from Hong Kong to Beijing. It was well past midnight and whatever hotels remained open were asking a king's ransom. We were on a budget so, for tonight at least, we opted to sleep under the stars.

The spring night made our little adventure comfortable, pleasant in fact. There had been mention of all-night vigils for the deceased Hu Yao Bang yet the streets in and around Tiananmen were deserted. Eventually we settled for a bench that looked out over a vast sweep of concrete known as Chang'an Avenue. There we lulled ourselves to sleep with talk of travel plans for the next month—the Great Wall, the Forbidden City, Xi'an's Terracotta Warriors, the sugarloaf mountains along the Li River, the Stone Forests of Kunming.

Around 4 a.m. we awoke to the din of distant shouting. As it grew in intensity so, it seems, did the anger. Soon the street was transformed into a riotous circus. The faces of young men and women lent expression to raucous chanting for "Reform! Reform! Reform!" From where we sat, their attention seemed riveted on a barely discernible line of green emerging from the far end of the avenue. Our curiosity turned to alarm as the line materialized into a wall of uniformed police. They easily numbered in the hundreds, advancing in purposeful, measured stride.

Fifty or so metres buffered the young protesters from the advancing security forces. This distance the students sought to maintain while launching a barrage of taunts. The response, however, bordered on disinterest, with only a handful of officers staging mock charges to keep the revellers "'honest." Or so it seemed.

It was only when the police had reached our vantage point that their tactics became apparent. Attention had been focussed away from the reserve patrols gathering at the opposite end of the avenue. The ambush revealed the ferocity behind the veneer of tolerance. The bravado turned to panic as students collapsed from repeated blows.

When dawn came, there was no sign of the human debris. April 19, 1989 would greet Beijing with blossoming lilacs, gentle breezes, warm sunshine. But beneath the surface were growing whispers of disaffection and tales of strange goings-on in the night. For China, it was the calm before the storm.

BY INVITATION

Al Purdy

THE VIRTUES OF SILENCE

I have never learned to keep my mouth shut—as my wife has sometimes pointed out. This is a basic flaw in my character, and more than once has proved dangerous.

Some twenty years ago I gave a reading in Halifax, afterwards attending a party hosted by the sponsors. I was warned in advance that I might be buttonholed by a pest my host called "the most boring man in Canada." Sure enough, I was and he was.

I can't remember what he looked like or his name, and after perhaps twenty minutes of listening to the guy's unending monologue I said in near desperation, "You're the most boring man in the world." And that was the end of that.

A dozen years ago I had another reading in Halifax, hosted by one Andy Wainwright. At my hotel before the reading a lady named Bonnie Purdy, who did interviews for the local television station, phoned me, and we talked about Purdy genealogy. She told me the last two Purdy males in the family had been nabbed by the English on the Scottish border and hanged for sheep stealing. Well, I said, or something like that. And the two Purdy sisters surviving—Bonnie Purdy went on—asked their husbands to take the name of Purdy, so the family wouldn't die out. And that accounts for you and I being here today. Well—it's a good story anyway.

I did the reading, and next day met Andy Wainwright at a pub as pre-arranged. From there we would drive to Halifax airport, and I would fly back home. But it turned out Andy didn't have time, had to teach a CanLit class or something. He'd arranged for someone else to take me instead. The "someone else" came by shortly and we started out for Halifax airport. Just as we were passing through one of those deep rock cuts in the highway my driver said: "Do you remember telling me I was the most boring man in the world?"

Glancing at the rock walls of the highway, it occurred to me that the dead bones of ancient sea creatures had once provided the ingredients for this limestone graveyard. I remained silent, the car's tires sounding abnormally loud.

The driver looked at me inquiringly. I avoided his eyes, staring straight ahead.

"Well, perhaps—" I started out.

Then: "Maybe I was—" But that wasn't right either.

Silence *fell*, and I mulled over the possibility that I might be making things worse than ever. If the driver completed those two beginnings of sentences, "Perhaps" and "Maybe," would there be any hope of a future life for me? One thing tho, he wasn't boring me.

If anyone reading this anecdote can tell me what I should have done on that awkward occasion, I'll reward them with a valuable prize. Perhaps. Maybe.

Charles S. Ross
"LAST HOLIDAY"

The scenario was a camping trip to Italy. The maternal grandmother, frail but energetic, had flown from Canada to Germany for a sojourn with daughter and family—her officer husband and two small grandchildren. Although quite elderly, she was a good sport and had condescended to accompany the foursome on a tenting foray to the hinterlands between Florence and Bologna. The outward journey was without incident, and a few days later they were at their destination. All seemed well, and even the children were adapted to their environment and enjoying themselves immensely.

The two younger generations used the main tent and grandmother slept in the smaller one, thus gaining a degree of privacy.

On the third morning, everyone else was up and about, but Grandma had failed to appear. When her daughter investigated, she was overwhelmed to find her dear mother had peacefully expired during the night. She was stone cold dead.

After the initial and devastating shock, the take-charge son-in-law, with military intuitiveness and fortitude, assessed the situation and confronted his wife with the cold facts. If the authorities were notified, then surely in true Italian fashion and red tape, Grandmother's last resting place would be this strange and distant land. However, if they could quietly get the old lady's remains back to Germany—he persuaded his wife—it would be clear sailing (flying) back to Canada. She hesitantly agreed, and quickly and reverently, the body was shrouded in the tent and placed securely on the top of the car for a quick exit from Italy.

That fateful morning they drove hard and fast, in silence, for 200 miles, but hunger and irritability overcame them and they stopped at a cafe to regroup and have lunch. That indeed must have been the most tasteless and disheartening meal they have ever had.

When they returned to the parking lot, their car was just as they had left it. Except for one thing: the small tent on the roof was missing.

I don't believe they have ever found Grandmother to this day.

Bernadette Rule

RANDOM AND DELIBERATE

In September of 1987 my brother Michael had heart surgery in Denver. Three days before he was to be flown home to Kentucky, my mother and I left his bedside to drive there with his belongings. We were relieved his ordeal was over, and my mother was especially glad he was retiring back home. Her only thought was to get there as quickly as possible and prepare him a comfortable welcome.

So it was that I came to be driving nonstop across stretches of the US I'd never seen before and longed to explore. The Sangre de Cristo Mountains strained the horizon as we drove south from Denver. But their very name set my mother musing on my brother's operation again, so at Pueblo I bore east into Kansas on Highway 50, turning away from New Mexico, perhaps forever.

There was nothing exotic about Kansas—small towns stamped with the featureless seal of the American midwest, landscape reduced to cash crops.

The sun set behind us and we pushed on into the gathering gloom. "We should start to look for a motel at the next town," said my mother. Almost immediately the road veered left and, on the curve, our headlights cut across the sign for Garden City. Of course, several motels were clustered at the edge of town. This predictability, which might have been comforting, oppressed me instead.

Mom does not enjoy travelling at the best of times, but anxiety caused her to fuss over details. She checked the bathroom suspiciously (for germs? cameras?) and pegged the slightly gaping curtains with three clothespins. Ready for bed by ten, she assured me the TV wouldn't bother her.

Random flipping turned up a special on Truman Capote. I had read and admired many of his short stories, but had assiduously avoided *In Cold Blood*, for the same reasons I had never read *Helter Skelter*. So I was completely startled to find the television screen replaying the drive I had just completed. The camera swung around the bend in the highway and cut across the sign for Garden City.

Scenes from the movie version of *In Cold Blood* followed—scenes of random and deliberate violence, shot on location, just off the highway outside of Garden City, Kansas. Beyond our pegged curtains, the darkened prairie breathed heavily.

Barry Ryce
ONE MOMENT, PLEASE

I was in Poona because of the war. A month previously we had flown our aircraft, a Wellington, from England, in a series of gentle hops, to Karachi, pre-independence India. Thirty flying hours; three weeks. No hurry; no *juldi*. Around the Bay of Biscay, across North Africa, tank tracks like spoors of animals clearly visible in the sand and then, like coloured pages of an atlas, the desolate browns of Arabia, Iran. At Karachi, as though we had been naughty boys, they took away our aircraft and sent us, by train, to Poona: to become acclimatized.

Poona, pucka Poona with its clubs for *burra sahibs*, its race course and, nearby the Aga Khan's Palace. There, behind the external splendour, Mahatma Gandhi was imprisoned. Gandhi had called for Home Rule, and for a time there had been a "Quit India" campaign and he had been detained in the palace. Saints are a terrible nuisance during a war.

Arriving at our living quarters just outside Poona, we did not know until midnight that we were to witness an unusual demonstration of tender support that Gandhi always inspired in people, not always Indian.

We lived in simple *basha* hut, pressure lamps for lighting, a table, a few chairs and the inevitable *charpoy* surmounted, like a joke four-poster, by a mosquito net. That first night everything felt strange but a more singular event was to happen. Somewhere a distant clock, like a town hall clock tower, struck the hours. You could hear it at night about the hiss of the pressure lamps and the pings of the flying beetles as they dashed themselves against the lamp glass. And then, at midnight when the clock struck twelve, in bed, against the stillness of the Poona night, we first heard the cry. A long drawn-out wail, G-a-an-d-h-i-i-i, so unexpected that it struck a chill down the spine. Then it was repeated, a long quavering forlorn cry. From how many throats? The cry of the people, the villagers I suppose; the call of children to their father, their *bapu*, expressing love, support, need. There was no anger, no fierceness in the sound. A curious moment in history. Poona, supposed bastion of the Raj; the Mahatma waiting with quiet disobedience; Indians crying out, in the middle of the night, a single word, Gandhi; and an air crew lying awake in a *basha*, not speaking, making no comment, wondering.

BY INVITATION

Chris Scott
FIRST CALVING

I awoke at 2:30 a.m. and wondered why my wife had set the alarm clock for that time. When the ring resolved into the telephone, I remembered that it was our first calving. Jodi, our Brown Swiss cow, had kept us up the night before with no result. It was her first calf too, and that would be my wife Heather calling from the barn.

"Chris, Jodi's uterus is all over the barn floor!"

"I'll come down," I said.

It was quite a sight, but at least I was prepared for it. Jodi lay on her side, hind legs sticking up in the air, her uterus a glistening mass the size of a large red wheelbarrow.

The calf was alive, and so was Jodi—but only just.

"Cover it with a towel," was the vet's advice (we didn't have one big enough), "and don't let her step on it."

When the vet arrived, he struggled into a novel designer garment, the sleeves joined by a great batwing rubber web. The idea was to catch the uterus in the web, then shove it back where it came from. A client had brought it back from Switzerland, the vet explained.

"She's only everted one horn of the uterus." He sounded disappointed as he cleaned Jodi's uterus, stripping away the placental membranes: "We'll soon have her put back together."

While he worked, he told this story about his first

103

calving. A young vet just out of school, he'd been called to a first calf heifer. "The calf was dead inside the birth canal and the cow was pretty torn up," the vet said, "and I had to take the calf to pieces. When I finally got it out, the mother cow looked done. 'I'm real sorry,' I told the farmer, 'but you might as well call the Purina factory.'"

The next day the vet was called to another calving—at a gas station. He delivered the calf safely. "Nice heifer," he complemented the owner. "Mind if I ask where you got her?"

"Driver of the Purina truck. She only cost a hundred bucks. Going to slaughter. I don't know why."

The vet did; it was the cow he had worked on the day before.

By now he'd finished pushing Jodi's uterus back up her vagina and stitching up her vulva.

"She had a calf in each horn," he said, straightening up. "I never did tell the owner of the gas station where she came from."

"And the farmer?" Heather asked.

"Hamburger, as far as he knew." The vet eyed his handiwork. Jodi was already struggling to her feet, nuzzling and licking her calf. "I'll just give her a shot of oxytocin and some penicillin. Take the stitches out in a week."

That was the next thing we had to learn—how to take stitches out of a cow's vulva.

Alice Seward
THE DAY I DIED

I can't forget the day I died,
And I shall not forget my guide!
He was a most unlikely guy
To lead a meek soul such as I.

It was a late October day.
I put my boring work away
To take a stroll through woodland fair,
For Autumn's glow was in the air.
The sun was warm, but the wind was cold
As maples shed their red and gold
Along the path I chose to take,
A sandy path above the lake.
From here I climbed a rocky hill;
The rocks were cold from Autumn's chill.

Narrow and steep the pathway grew
And night was not far off, I knew;
I told myself I'd turn back soon,
And presently a great white moon
Rose from behind another hill,
Showing the cold rocks white and still.
I turned and started to descend,
But took the path that has no end.
Down, up, and down again I went,
In soul and body, sorely spent.

And now and then I leaned my weight
Against a rock, cursing the fate
That sent me on this crazy jaunt,

These cold and cheerless hills to haunt.
One rock I sat on in this place
Appeared to have a lion's face.
Too weary to be shocked at such
A flagrant incongruity,
I sighed, "Thank God!" and presently
The lion turned and looked at me.

His eye was green and cold and wide,
My chilling fear I could not hide!
He whispered, "Stop, you're killing me!
Your weight's too much for my old side."
I quickly rose, shook off my fear,
For I was lost and night was near;
Unless this lion were my friend
I knew I soon should meet my end.
The lion stretched in every limb,
But I was not afraid of him.

And then I heard a fearful screech
And something splashed upon the beach.
I looked toward the sands below,
So near, and yet so far to go,
And in the moon's erratic glow,
People were rushing to and fro.
A prostrate figure, people bent
On taking in the accident.
I said, "There's something wrong below."
The lion said, "I fear 'tis so."

"There's someone hurt—I wonder who?"
The lion yawned, "I fear 'tis you;
The word is not 'hurt', as you said—
Somebody down there says you're dead."
And then he roared, "The gods are dumb,
They might have plucked a choicer plum,

But now there's just that mixed-up stew
Of unconnected things called YOU.
Somebody stirred the pot too soon,
Congealed the mass, and lost the spoon;
But where's the hand that stirred the pot?
It's too late now, the thing's too hot!''

"But I shall lead you—have no fear—
Your Home is not too far from here.''
Somewhere a strange voice called my name,
And life has never been the same.

Royal W. Shepard
OLD TOM'S SWAN SONG

He was a large turkey, large enough to take comfort in the thought that it would have to be a great occasion, with many guests, for a bird of his stature to grace the table. He survived the first encounter with the snake, but lost to Aunt Hannah's wrath.

It was mid-morning on a glorious summer day. I was sitting on the front porch spying on the hummingbirds neck-deep in the trumpet like flowers on the morning glory vine. Aunt Hannah was in the garden picking peas for supper. She spoke, "What's the matter with you?"

There was no answer, then after a few seconds, a despairing cry, "Lord God have mercy. You'll choke to death you old fool. Let go. Let go, I say.''

I ran around the house to the garden to witness a

bizarre scene—a tug-of-war. The old turkey had a snake—much too large a snake, partially swallowed. Aunt Hannah, with her feet also firmly planted, had a tight grip on the snake's tail.

Old Tom didn't have a chance. He was tiring rapidly and short of breath. Aunt Hannah moved slowly backward, admonishing the old fool to let go. He braced himself; let his feet dig a furrow for a few feet, and suddenly disgorged the snake. The old lady tumbled backward and disappeared behind the pea vines. Her remarks withered three rows of yellow beans.

Instead of making tracks for the safety of the barnyard or the pasture, Old Tom strutted over to the spot where Aunt Hannah had vanished. He stretched his long neck over the pea vine and looked down at his prostrate foe. He savoured the sight for some seconds, then threw back his head and gave a victory gobble. Still clutching the snake's tail, the old lady scrambled to her feet. She cut short his bugling with a mighty roundhouse swing. The snake caught the old warrior on the side of the head. With that one blow she killed the turkey and the snake.

It was the toughest meat I ever blunted my teeth on. We ate the turkey for many days in many—I could not count the ways.

Art Sissons
TAKEN

My grandfather considered himself to be an excellent horse trader and an honourable man. He was also my buddy and we told each other tales. His stories were far better than mine, and here is a favourite that he told to me:

"A scoundrel owed me some money and couldn't pay me, so I accepted a pit bull from him to settle the debt. The dog was magnificent and I thought he would make an excellent watchdog. He would have, except for one fault which I was not told about: he hated horses and attacked them whenever he could. Since I always kept horses, I had no choice but to get rid of him.

"But what could I do? He was a great-looking dog and I did not want him destroyed, but he was well-known and no one wanted to buy him. He was too good to put down, and besides, I needed to recoup my losses on this deal.

"I was reading my newspaper one morning and saw an item in the barter column:

Will trade: One four-year-old gelding, properly broken to light harness, some Morgan blood. For a sound pit bull. Apply P.O. Box 123, Rocky Mountain House, Alberta.

"I couldn't wait on the postal service, I sent a telegram that same morning:

Have sound three-year-old pit bull   stop   Will trade stop   Request prompt reply   stop

"I received a reply that day:

Accepted   stop   Letter to follow   stop.

"A week later, the letter arrived. It enclosed a photograph of a truly beautiful horse, harnessed to a surrey. The letter said:

This is the horse. Sorry, surrey not included. What do you think?

"I thought that I should make a deal and sent a letter back saying so.

"We agreed and the deal was done."

My grandfather paused, and then continued in a very serious tone.

"Two weeks later I read the story in the newspaper about a dog in Rocky Mountain House running a team of horses off the road. It reported that the driver had jumped to save his life, and that the team was injured and had to be destroyed. It went further and said that the dog had been ordered shot, and it mentioned the owner's name. It was the man who had gotten the dog from me. I've regretted that deal to this day, and wish that I had not left out the horse-chasing part when I described the dog."

"Did that man ever get back to you about it?" I wanted to know.

"No," he drawled. "He never did."

And that is the story I was told when I was fifteen, and until one Sunday afternoon, when I was twenty-three, I thought it was the whole story.

At that time I took my grandfather out for a drive in his old Chev sedan. While we were parked at a favourite spot, overlooking a local riding stable, he actually finished the story.

"When I told you the story about the dog that I traded for a horse, I didn't tell you everything.

"The whole story is, that the horse I got from Rocky Mountain House was . . ." My grandfather looked away, out the car window.

"Was what, Grandpa?"

"Was . . ." He still wasn't looking at me.

"WAS WHAT, GRANDPA?!" I raised my voice.

"Well . . . hewasblind!"

"What?!"

"HE WAS BLIND!! . . . TOTALLY! . . . COMPLETE-LY! . . . BLIND!!"

Dennis Slater
SOULSCAPES

Wind snapped at the worn trees—silent crones in a stone-littered yard. Near ruined walls, gnarled plants stretched and clung to rock-bound wood in an ancient tower. I ran from the rain, its bite hounding my hands, neck, cheek and lips. A broken flagstone clung to ground at a rakish angle. Its sharp edge caught my heel and cast me near cold rotted wood. It was a courtyard circled with the bent back of a stone fence.

I looked at the gaping mouth of the old tower yawning at time and tempest. It was like a dream—fog sliding along wet grass, rain crying from stone and tree. Suddenly, black sound leapt from an ancient tree and wheeled and circled near my head. A strange chill crept past my heart and stirred in my eyes. The crow cawed once, wheeled, cawed, and swung back to a tree branch. Wind rocked the branch beneath it, rain railed around it, but no feather stirred. Apparition? I wished yes, but black wings tore air again. It cawed and circled and cawed and circled and I closed my eyes.

That was five years ago in that wind-tossed yard, and rain still rends stone in my memory. My people were superstitious and that chain still binds part of me. The crow paints the air with its wings, beats the rain, and circles the tower. My grandmother was a great one for omens. Birds hitting windows bring death. What about the ones circling round you in the rain? Well, grandmother really didn't address that one. But folklore of the Irish variety gives part of the answer. It's even more disturbing than the buffeting of wings in my dreams.

They say witches could assume the shapes of birds

111

and animals and black isn't a good colour in anybody's book. They also say the dead come in birds as soul carriers. Sounds like it's stretching it? Well maybe, or so my wife says. None of this Celtic nonsense in someone so young.

Have you ever felt that way? Felt that you see it. It's a bird, right? Try it sometime in the rain in an ancient courtyard. Stand on the sodden leaves and slide on sharp rock. Try it. Is the inky voice speaking to you or maybe warning you? Or is it just a bird fighting wind and rain? Aren't we all prisoners when the reason light shorts out? Think about it.

Helen Somers
THE OLD MAN

After Father recovered from his stroke, he would sit on his doorstep and wait and listen, and in the twilight he walked his fields. Father said he was watching and waiting for his old man.

One evening I joined him on his doorstep and he told me the story of what happened to him last spring.

It was a chilly morning in April and the warmth from the heater felt good as he stepped into the idling pickup truck. The sun was shining. He settled himself on the seat, put the truck in gear and drove off. He had three calls to make for the agriculture company he worked for.

Traffic was heavy and he was glad the truck was running well. He had driven about twenty-five miles when his head began to feel light, then he got dizzy. His vision blurred. He couldn't see the centre line. He became confused, and he forgot where he was going. He was frightened. "Oh, Lord, help me," he exclaimed. He was afraid he would run off the road or strike another car.

All at once he realized he was not alone. He looked over and saw an old man sitting on the seat beside him.

The old man was handsome. Stockily built, with wide shoulders, a ruddy face, brown eyes and a cleft in his chin. He was wearing working clothes, black and red mackinaw coat and wide-brimmed hat.

Dad recognized him. It was his father. Dad said in relief, "Am I ever glad to see you!"

The old man replied, "Calm down, I'll help you. Take your foot off the gas, and pull over at the next driveway, then turn your truck around." That's what my dad did.

The old man then said, "Stop at this house just ahead, the people who live there know you and will help you."

Father was so confused he didn't remember who lived there. He turned to ask the old man to come into the house with him, but the old man had disappeared. The Smiths, who lived in the house, did not see anyone with Dad when he drove in.

The Smiths took Dad to hospital, where the doctor said he had suffered a stroke.

The old man, my grandfather, had died thirty years before this event. Did his ghost come back to help my father, or was he an angel?. . . It cannot be explained.

Margaret Sorensen
HELP ON THE ROAD

It was May 16th of this year, the second day of the Ontario truckers' highway blockade. I was driving from London, Ontario, to Listowel and listening to Vicky Gabereau's radio program. An intriguing Anecdote Contest in support of Canada–India assistance was being described. While it occurred to me that nothing interestingly anecdotal had happened to me within recent memory, still the cause was appealing and the suggested donation of $5.00 one I could afford.

Little realizing that I was already in the midst of an anecdote, I pulled off to the side of the road to await the repetition of the contest address. Just as I settled myself with pen and paper, a large transport truck pulled to the side of the road, squarely in front of me. My first thought-flash was, "Good grief, am I to suffer a personal truck blockade?" At which I stepped out on the road as did the trucker and we met at a democratic halfway point. "Your car is in trouble?" was the gentle accusation. "No, no, my car is OK." My denial carried all the conviction of one who had recently paid $1,300 for a complete car fix-up. I explained about the contest, apologized for the bother and warmly thanked the would-be rescuer: "How great that someone would care enough to stop to help." Then, my scanty knowledge of the truckers' grievances notwithstanding, I cried after his retreating figure, "And I support the truckers!"

The truck moved on. Having successfully recorded the contest address, I, too, proceeded on my way—for about ten miles that is—when I was obliged to pull to the side of the road as my car hysterically coughed itself to a standstill . . . signalling, for heaven's sake, the demise of its fuel filter.

Tim Sullivan
LIFE'S SIMPLE PLEASURES

The value of money has certainly diminished over recent years. Nonetheless, if one is placed in the right circumstances, a great deal of happiness can be bought with a single dollar!

About ten years ago we spent an extended summer season as low-echelon employees at a luxurious resort in the Canadian Rockies. We accepted our modest wage in exchange for the "life experience"—and that it was. Many a payday found us in the local town consuming comfort foods to compensate for staff rations, and buying various items to liven up our barren quarters. It never took long for the money to disappear.

One Sunday we set out for the afternoon with nothing in our pockets but a free pass for two up a nearby mountain tramway. We hitchhiked to the site, boarded the cable car and rode to the top, content to pass the time climbing and enjoying the view from above.

After a rather steep hike on the rocky terrain, we paused for a rest on some boulders. By this time we'd grown tired, hungry and thirsty; contentment was slipping from our grasp. Our hearts grew heavy with the reminder that we were penniless; we sat apart, isolated in our own despairs. Loneliness, frustration; the simple wish to be a carefree tourist . . .

With a sudden outburst she broke my contemplative spell—Come quickly! Look what I've just found!!! While kicking the rocks at her feet, her bored gaze had focussed on a small piece of crumpled paper. She'd reached down to retrieve it and discovered to her amazement that it was a very old, dirty, tattered dollar bill!! There is no way to describe the incredible wealth and good fortune we felt at that point. A nod from our friend Fate!! We hurried down the slope to the teahouse and spent our dollar as wisely as we could on two warm, freshly baked chocolate chip cookies and a glass of milk to share between us. Nothing had ever tasted as wonderful as those cookies—and the milk was incredibly cold and thirst-quenching—denial must have enhanced the taste.

Temporarily rejuvenated, we returned to the tram and descended the mountain to our place among the affluent, and to reality . . .

BY INVITATION

Julian Symons
SHARPNESS OF EYE

In the Thirties, Roy Fuller, Herbert Mallalieu and I went on holiday together, three young poets plus two wives (I was unmarried) and two small children. It was a seaside holiday at a place called St. Mary's Bay in Kent, which Kate warned us (rightly) was "bleak, flat and unromantic." We played paper games, read poetry aloud, did a lot of swimming. One incident while we were swimming established Roy permanently in my mind as not merely a keen observer, but almost a magician.

As a result of boxing without a gum shield in adolescence, I had loosened two front teeth, which eventually had to be replaced by a small plate. When swimming I swallowed a mouthful of sea water, coughed, gulped, expelled the plate and emerged horribly gap-toothed.

Ducking and diving underwater proved useless. A few hours later, with the tide out, Fuller, Mallalieu and I wandered, hopelessly as I felt, about the stony beach looking for the tiny plate. But—I can hardly believe it even now—after several minutes Roy gave a cry and held up the sea-washed teeth, returned by the tide to almost exactly the area of beach where I had lost them. Since then I have always believed that it must be possible to find a needle in a haystack.

David Thomas

THE ACQUIRING OF NUMBER TWENTY-THREE

Marsh Mews was a coy name for a row of pretentious houses erected too quickly to cover a cheaply acquired swamp. Cynical locals called it Bog Folly.

That is why number twenty-three was desirable. It stood on a little knoll, looking down smugly and drily upon its bog-bound neighbours. My father lusted after it. In waterproof boots he would wallow in our lawn at number twenty-two and mutter, "If ever they move . . ."

When war broke out, we dutifully accepted gas masks and air raid warnings. Although the big seaport, thirty miles away, was devastated by enemy bombing, our village seemed safe, and after some initial enthusiasm we paid scant attention to precautions enjoined upon us by the government.

But the Maggses, in number twenty-three, took war seriously. Their house became as near a fortress as any villa-in-a-row could ever become. Doors were protected by walls of sandbags. Lower windows were shielded by galvanized metal, and uppers were criss-crossed by adhesive tape. Fire buckets shared hallways with water pumps and shovels. At the heart of the house, in the morgue of a dining room, was a huge table shelter constructed of heavy steel and wire mesh.

It was into this that the ample Mrs. Maggs squeezed herself, with leverage provided by her husband, whenever a siren sounded. For comfort, she took with her a flask of tea, some digestive biscuits and a budgie in its cage . . . a double imprisonment that was to prove tragic.

118

Ironically, the only bomb to fall on our village was dropped by a stray aircraft into the back garden of number twenty-three. The only damage it did was to splatter the neighbourhood with mud. But its terrifying bang caused Mrs. Maggs to choke on a mouthful of biscuit. Gasping her last, she attempted to get up. Instead, she fell backwards and sat on the unfortunate budgie, whose war ended right there.

Mr. Maggs moved away shortly afterwards, to live with his unmarried sister. And so it was that we acquired number twenty-three. The hole in the back garden quickly filled with water and my father bought some ducks, to supplement our egg and meat ration. We never did use the dining room. My mother swore she could taste feathers.

Colleen E. Thornhill

WAS IT ONLY A DREAM?

There is a story that has haunted my memory for many years and still comes back to my conscious mind at the most unexpected times. After all this time, I can still summon a shiver about it. I was just a young child when I overheard my aunt tell of the experience but the obvious wonder and awe in her voice sent chills through me—children know the ring of truth when they hear it!

This is her story as she told it to the family at breakfast the morning after it happened.

"I had a weird dream last night. It was so vivid, so real, so frightening! I dreamt that I had awakened and something was drawing me to sit up. I did and then, still with that sensation of being drawn forward, I found myself putting on my stockings. Everything seemed to move so slowly and so deliberately.

"After I had pulled on my stockings, I was impelled to stand up—again, slowly and in a dreamlike manner. Then I turned and knew that I was to go out of the room. The act of moving was effortless, although very slow, because I seemed to be floating over the floor. My feet were not touching at all but rather felt as though I was standing in deep cotton wool.

"As I turned, I caught a glimpse of myself in the mirror. It was ghastly! I was whiter than white—ghost-like, if you will—and my eyes were wide open and staring. I looked so . . . different, somehow. In fact, the eerie apparition in the mirror that was myself was so alarming that I was released from whatever power was controlling me and quickly hopped back into bed, pulling the covers tight around me.

"The dream was so strong and so much with me that when I woke this morning, it was the first thing that came to me. I could still feel the chill of that ghostly figure in the mirror!

"When I finally managed to shake off the fear, I threw the covers back and got out of bed.

"To my horror, I saw that I was wearing my stockings and they certainly had not been on my legs when I went to bed!!"

Valerie Walia

A ROOM FOR THE NIGHT

My brother and his family took a vacation in France. They picked up their rental car at the airport and followed a route that would take them out of the city toward a small town where they could find a hotel for the night. As the effects of jet lag set in, Tom presently found himself the only one in the car still awake. By this time he was feeling decidedly weary himself and decided to head for the first hotel he could find. Accordingly, he followed a series of well-marked signs and eventually pulled into the parking lot of a substantial hotel building near the city centre. Feeling pleased with himself, he went inside and asked for accommodation for a family of four.

The lady at the desk understood his request and handed him a registration form to complete. She gestured him to a booth with a table and chair and he sat down to fill out the form. He soon realized why the chair and table were provided; the form was in fact a two-page questionnaire of considerable detail. It required all the help he could get from his phrase-book, and some of the questions confounded him. Finally it was done, signed and handed back to the receptionist. Tom hurried triumphantly to the car to bring in the suitcases and the rest of the family.

The sleepy occupants of the car gathered their various baggage and pushed through the heavy doors into the lobby. Sleepy they may have been, but even so, they realized at once that something about the hotel Tom had booked for them was not quite right. A look of incredulity passed across the face of the receptionist, followed by a hearty burst of laughter. Co-workers were summoned from a back room and the joke shared with them before explanations were finally relayed to the bewildered family.

"Monsieur, the form you have filled out is not for a hotel room!"

Too late the realization flashed into Tom's brain. Of course l'Hôtel de Ville was not a hotel. It was the Town Hall and he had just filled out an application form for public housing!

BY INVITATION

David Watmough

AUTHOR-ARSONIST

While perceived primarily as an author in Canada, for the past quarter of a century I've been alternatively known to two of my closest friends as an arsonist, bankrupter or worse. This is the result of certain activities along the Connecticut Valley and amid the scattered hill towns of the Berkshires in western Massachusetts.

In 1965 when celebrating my fortieth birthday, I was unduly pensive while in the Tod Morden restaurant near Goshen, Massachusetts. That was because I was contemplating middle age and not for thinking I might be an unwitting conduit of malevolent forces. Only in a subsequent letter was I informed the restaurant had mysteriously burned down shortly after my visit.

The following year I was shocked to learn that a secondhand bookstore in the town of Pittsfield had closed within days of my perusing its shelves. Only later, after many more such collapses and conflagrations, did I start to ponder my powers and flirt with unsettling conclusions.

By the time I visited Hadley, site of Mt. Holyoke College, I was getting into my stride. After two trips to The Odyssey, a bookstore of eminent reputation, the place burned down twice!

It was also in Hadley that an architecturally intriguing restaurant fell victim to closure shortly after my patronage. The service was slow—but surely not tardy enough to stem my rising unease at what looked less and less like synchronicity and more and more like psychic extravagance.

In neighbouring Northampton, home of Smith College, I "took care" successively of Beardley's and Proto Fino, after dining in them, and the Albion Bookstore, which closed as precipitately after I had visited it, as both restaurants had gone up in smoke.

Remotely situated outside the village of Ashfield there once flourished a gourmet's delight called The New Hope. It was greatly prized and could afford to only open a few days each week. Soon after a single visit from me those few days were reduced to none.

It is evident that although content with my avowals of powerlessness over whatever I activate in my wake, my hosts are now cautious about where they take me on my annual visitation. We eschew their favorite places.

I also have learned to be circumspect when visiting restaurants and bookstores in the Berkshires. If I cannot spy a fire extinguisher or if I hear the mildest complaints about lack of business, I flee.

Dolores Ruth Wilkins
DINNER DATE WITH PETER GOE

The Captain waved to the shipping company's personnel manager, then entered his office.

"I don't believe you've met my wife, Mr. Goe."

"No Captain—"

The phone jangled. "Wait, Captain, will you and your wife join me for supper tonight at Fosters?"

"Mr. Goe seems nice," I said as we walked out of the building.

"Yes, but crews don't think so. Our crew had to kick back their first two months' wages to Peter Goe."

"Poor men."

"Only yesterday he had to fire an oiler whose incompetence was a hazard. The whole office could hear the oiler threatening Goe harm if he did not return the 'kickback' and pay him his wages. Goe refused. The oiler shrieked that Goe had better have the money ready when he returned."

"So Goe is two-faced?"

"Unfortunately this is the custom. Goe's own wages are minimal, so it's his way of surviving. But no one likes his rice bowl threatened, so the oiler was pretty upset."

In this warehouse area, away from fashionable Orchard Road, Singapore was a city of smells. Although rectangles of cement straddling open sewers were being replaced, their odors still blended with aromas of curries, coriander, cinnamon and cloves.

We walked along the Singapore River, saddened to see that the picturesque dwellings lining the embankment were being demolished. Tucked between two of these houses was a tiny temple, where joss sticks burned in a brass bowl. Outside, hardly noticeable among the warehouse boxes, was a crate confining a boa constrictor. This temple was his, for he was the River Dragon.

We ate banana fritters from a Malaysian cart, inspected Indonesian puppets, Sri Lankan demon cups, mirrored elephants and alabaster Taj Mahals from India, until we realized that we might be late for supper. The

Captain decided to phone Peter Goe, to apologize for our possible delay.

"He may still be at the office, I'll check.

"Hello, has Mr. Goe left yet? May I speak with him, please?

"Dial tone! That's strange, all I heard was a secretarial gasp. The nerve, she hung up on me."

As it turned out, there had been a reason for the secretarial gasp. The oiler had returned. Goe still refused to pay him. The oiler pulled a bearing scraper from a paper bag and stabbed him.

Goe died, right there in the office.

The Captain phoned.

We never did have dinner with Peter Goe.

Doreen Wilson
SHOCK

Quite a number of years ago, my husband was travelling in the Gaspé, on business. It was dark, pitch black, when he checked into a fishing lodge for the night. Exhausted from a long drive, he stripped off all his clothes and fell thankfully into bed.

In the morning when he awoke, the sun was streaming through the old closed, wooden louvred doors. Feeling great, he jumped out of bed, still in the "altogether," and threw open the floor-to-ceiling doors as wide as possible, stretching his arms wide and yawning hugely, eyes closed.

When he opened his eyes, he saw to his horror, about twenty feet away, the stunned faces of the diners on the Old Ocean Ltd. train, which was standing still on the track.

"It was a heart-sinking moment," he remembers, "and I can still to this day see the horrified faces of those people in the dining car, coffee cups suspended in mid-air while I—naked as a newborn babe—gaped at them, like the village idiot."

Oh, the joys of travel.

Judy Winter
UNCHARTED PATHS

In 1957, when I was five years old and my sister was six, my parents, Erik and Ellen Watt, took us on a 1200-mile journey in a fourteen-foot outboard down the Mackenzie River to Aklavik, sixty miles south of the Arctic Ocean. We were the first, and perhaps still the only white family, to make the journey in a small open boat.

After several lonely days of travel through the wilderness, we were surprised to see a kayak ahead of us, rigged with a sail. The man and woman paddling it were awkwardly out of synch. When we pulled up beside them, my father introduced us and asked them if they need a hand.

"Thank you," replied the young man with a formal German accent. "I would be very pleased if you could tell us where we are." He held up a small map so my father could show him where they were. The entire Mackenzie River route was twelve inches long, about an eighth as large as one of our seven river charts.

The young German couple were newlyweds, and

127

kayaking on the Yukon gold rush route was the husband's idea of an exciting honeymoon. His young wife, sitting stiffly in the kayak, kept smiling at us but looked quite miserable.

"We tried to use our sail on the river but our kayak turned over," the young man said.

We offered them some of our food, but they had no room to carry it. They were relying on reaching settlements and buying food along the way. Their food supply consisted of black bread, cheese and lard.

Before we parted company we took pictures of each other. My father promised them that he would tell the RCMP at the next settlement to watch out for the German couple in case they ran into trouble.

"That poor woman," my mother said afterwards. "I hope they make it." We never saw them again.

In the summer of 1961, my father's cousin, Nick Radford, was hitchhiking on the autobahn north of Frankfurt. He was happy to be picked up by a couple in a Volkswagen minibus, all fitted out for camping. They spoke English well and told Nick about their recent mountain-climbing adventures in Iceland and Nepal. When they discovered Nick lived in Edmonton, they began to talk excitedly about their northern adventure in 1957.

"That's the same summer my cousins went down the Mackenzie River!" Nick said. "They took their three daughters."

"Do you mean the Watts?" they exclaimed in unison.

John Windsor
THE PHANTOM OF TEXARKANA

It was Friday, September 13, 1946 and my wife Pam and I, together with our two-year-old daughter Jane, were driving from Kingston to Vancouver. Our route led southwest through Arkansas toward the Texas border, which we reached about ten o'clock that night. The border was straddled by a small town called Texarkana. Its main street was made bright as day by garishly lit store windows. However, there was one thing that was strange. The town seemed to be deserted, and it appeared we were the only living creatures left.

As we drove away I rolled up my window to light a cigarette and at the same time Pam had rolled up hers. Our car was old and the engine was badly overheated, and suddenly, as both windows went up, a great gush of heat seemed to pour into the car.

"Oh my God, we're on fire," was our first thought. I jammed on the brakes and, hastily scooping up Jane, we abandoned the vehicle and stood watching and waiting. But nothing happened. Finally we calmed down, realizing that closing both windows had caused the sudden heat. We were both tired and decided to go no farther that night.

As there was no ditch, we drove the car onto the flat prairie and then hauled out our bedrolls; spreading them out on the side removed from the road, we settled down to sleep. The last thing I remember before drifting off was hearing a vehicle coming down the road. It was driving slowly and as it came abreast of us, it halted.

Then for a full minute, though it seemed longer, the driver of the other car inspected ours. Finally he must have decided it was deserted and drove off. A few moments later I was fast asleep. It was only a minor misadventure, and early the following morning we were on our way to Vancouver.

A number of weeks later I heard Pam, who had been glancing idly through an old copy of *Life* magazine, suddenly gasp.

"Listen to this," she said. It was a report on a maniacal murderer who had been dubbed the Phantom Killer of Texarkana. Apparently this madman killed at random in or near the town, but only on Friday nights. On August the twenty-third he shot and killed a young couple sitting in a parked car and on the following Friday night he killed another young couple also in their car. Then on Friday September the sixth he had killed a farmer and seriously wounded his wife as they sat in their kitchen.

By this time the whole town and district were in a stage of panic with the inhabitants sitting armed in their darkened homes in case the killer should attack them. The article ended with the frightening question, "Will the phantom strike again on Friday September the thirteenth?"

That was the night we had slept unprotected outside the town. Had it been the Phantom who stopped his car and surveyed ours in the hope of finding a couple sitting there? Unable to locate a copy of a later magazine, we never did find the answer to that question or whether he had murdered again that night.

BY INVITATION

George Woodcock

A MATTER OF NAMES

Kathmandu, early 1970. We had gone to Nepal to investigate the condition of Tibetan refugees there, and were feeling oppressed by the claustrophobic atmosphere of the little capital, more infested then by spies than any place I have known. One Sunday, as an outing, a relief worker we had met offered to take us up the new road the Chinese had been building from Kathmandu to the Tibetan border. When he came in his Volkswagen Beetle, it struck me that he seemed somewhat exalted (hash was cheaper and abundant then) but we drove off in great style out of the valley of Kathmandu and northward through the mountain passes.

In Nepal, when a truck breaks down, the driver will usually leave a few rocks around it to warn oncoming traffic to detour. After an hour we came to such an arc of stones from which the truck had gone, and to my surprise, instead of swerving, our friend drove straight at it, and rending metal screamed under the car. We stopped to look; a steady stream of oil was trickling out.

A car of Nepalis stopped; they suggested we ask for help at the Chinese road-building depot up the highway. We drove to it. Men were sitting in the compound under a vast portrait of Mao Tsetong, and a soldier appeared at the gate. Our friend spoke to him in Nepali; he made an impatient signal and waved his automatic rifle menacingly. We drove off; later I learned we had got off lightly;

the Canadian High Commissioner was stoned at the same spot and Frank Moraes, the Delhi journalist, was beaten and his photographer's camera smashed.

By now the oil was rapidly emptying. Luckily, a village potter appeared, carrying terra-cotta bowls in a great rope net on his back. We stopped him, bought a shallow vessel and a bit of string, and somehow tied it on so that it received at least part of the drip; twice we emptied what had accumulated into the oil tank as we made out our way back to the valley, freewheeling down the hills.

At last we reached the outskirts of the old town of Bhatgaon, east of Kathmandu, and saw a gas station just outside the walls. A great sign advertised Mobiloil. We drove in and asked for oil. "Sorry, no oil!" Disaster! The stock must have run dry! "But what about your advertisement?" I asked angrily. "Ah, sahib," said the attendant condescendingly, "you asked for *oil. We* sell *Mobiloil*." I should, I have since realized, have sold the story to the oil company's advertising agents. But my presence of mind operates on a primitive level—such as terra-cotta pots!

Caroline Woodward

THAT EYE STORY OF JACK'S

At the station in Watson Lake (1939) there was a fella who was gradually going mad, with an atrocious thing in his head. It started off as an infected sinus and instead of being able to burst its way out, it went inward . . . toward his brain. For weeks he could do nothing but pace and he couldn't understand anything you said to him. Watson Lake wasn't frozen enough to get a ski-plane in on it and it was too frozen to get a floatplane down on it. It got to the point where I was terrified he was going to die on me . . . So I got through on the radio to Fort St. John, to Dr. Kearney. He told me I'd have to open up this thing or else he'd die. He promised to come out to the radio station that night when the reception was better and he would guide me. He told me to get a razor blade and break it so it would have a diagonal break with a piercing and a cutting edge. He asked me to sterilize it and to get lots of sterile cloth ready and to tie him down . . . No anaesthetic. Not even whisky around!

At eight o'clock that night, Charlie Lake (940 km away) came in and Doctor Kearney was there. The young fella was like a log in the chair. All right, Kearney says, you gotta begin cutting and there's gonna be lots of blood so don't be afraid of it. Just mop it up but you got to cut deep. I started . . . I had to cut right beside his eye toward the bridge of his nose. It bled and I felt him wince a little but I held his head and cut and cut. My hand was shaking, believe me . . . It took the longest time but finally I pierced through. Kearney said it's gonna come out and it won't be very nice. I had a pan there and this decomposed matter came out in a gush, pretty near half a cup. He flopped, fainted. I told Kearney and he said, "So far so good. I think everything may be all right then. Make him up a bed there and put him face down and let that drain." The young fella slept for thirty hours! I thought he was dead a few times. When he finally woke up, he said, "Well! I'm hungry!" He hadn't eaten for about a week. But he was feeling good, his headache was gone and this thing, it drained for about four days and then it quit and knit. When I got him out about three

133

weeks later on a ski-plane, Kearney took a look at it and said we couldn't have done better here in the hospital!

Now there was another time Vic Johnson made a magnet out of copper wire wound around and around and laid across a six-volt battery and I pulled a piece of steel out of a guy's eye, about an eighth of an inch long it was. That time worked out fine too. But there's nothing like the first incident where I had to cut the guy, go right in and cut.

(Aural History Project: North Peace River. Subject: Jack Baker)

BY INVITATION

Eric Wright
THE OTTAWA RUN

On a hot, hot day in June I flew to Ottawa from Toronto to get a visa for a visit to Russia. I had spent a week on the telephone, until finally the consul said, "No more conversations. Come to Ottawa."

So I did, carrying my passport, thirty dollars and two photographs. "You need an official invitation," the consul said. "From Moscow." I had one, back in Toronto.

I spent two hours in the Novosti press agency getting a copy of the official invitation and ran back to the consul. "Now you need three photographs," he said. "Won't two do?" I pleaded. "I'm supposed to leave tomorrow." "We require three," he said.

I raced around some back streets until I found a cab and explained my problem to the driver.

"There's one in the mall," the cabbie said. "Right behind McDonald's. But I can't get in because it's a one-way street, so I'll come up the back of Ogilivie's, you go through the store, across the street, through McDonald's and there's a photographer right behind it. Okay?"

It was now twelve-thirty. At a dead run, sweating heavily (the temperature was ninety and the humidity was typical for Ottawa), I followed his directions, got my three pictures and raced back to the consulate, which was closed. It opened again at three.

Time for lunch. I found an Italian restaurant and ate a sandwich at a sidewalk table. Still with some Russian time to spare I went for a stroll. I had gone about twenty yards when a man stepped out from behind a tree. Could he have a word with me? Who was he? He flashed a card. The secret service. Ours. I had been picked up and I hadn't even got to Moscow yet.

At my suggestion we went for a beer (which I made him pay for) and he explained that he was curious as to why I had made so many visits to the consulate that day. I explained my mission—I had been invited to represent Canada at a conference of crime writers in Yalta. I think my trade made him nervous, but eventually he was satisfied, and we had a nice chat about spying.

As we finished our beer, I began to wonder how he had found me on that particular stretch of road, and then I realized. It was irresistible. "You were tailing me, weren't you?" I said. "Then, when I doubled back across the park and caught a cab and ducked through Ogilivie's and went in and out of McDonald's, I shook you, didn't I? Didn't I? And then you found me again sitting having lunch on the sidewalk, so you went behind that tree and waited for me? Right?"

He didn't actually blush, but his laugh was a bit strained. "No, no," he said. "I've been seeing you around all day. I just thought I'd have a word."

He did lose me, though. And if I ever get into writing spy novels, I have the scene of the Ottawa chase already written, as long as that street is still one way.

BY INVITATION

Ronald Wright

KANGAROO

In the Outback a few hundred miles from Alice Springs, there's a little bar which has a billiard table and a ceiling festooned with the underpants of those who have wagered their shorts and lost. It isn't the sort of place you'd expect to meet Canadians, but when I was settling the day's dust with a chilled tube, in walked Jurgen and Floyd: two men with prairie accents and one jacket between them; two men visibly shaken. They were realtors from a place called Product, Sask. The Outback, they said, hadn't intimidated them until today. They liked plenty of driving and plenty of sky. Mountains and trees spoiled the view. The thousand-mile asphalt bootlace tying Alice Springs to Adelaide hadn't seemed much hotter than the TransCanada in August. Best of all it had no speed limit. Floyd had been driving, and as fast as he liked: 180, 190, 200 . . . What was that in miles per hour? The trip was his treat, thanks to a big sale, and he was determined to enjoy it. Each fall for twenty-seven years, he and Jurgen had stalked moose and drunk beer together in the muskeg. They had beer with them in the car (nothing unlawful about that here), a couple of dozen sitting in a cooler like ammunition in a clip. Every half hour, Floyd's hand groped behind the seat and pried loose another one.

"Wasn't gettin drunk or nothin," he insisted. The beer kept his mouth wet, but that was about all: the

137

desert air, breathing in the windows like a dragon, sucked the alcohol from his pores as fast as he could get it down. He was thinking about moose: he'd miss them this year. Some people said a camel was a horse designed by a committee, but surely they were wrong. It had to be a moose.

Moose don't hop, Floyd had almost had time to remind himself, when a brownish shape leapt from a clump of mulga bush. He hit the brakes and the desert slowed down, but animal and car were destined to meet.

The impact woke Jurgen from a snooze. The two got out. They looked at the steam escaping from the radiator, and at the soft white fur on the belly of the weird creature lying on the road. Funny how the Aussies shortened everything. This wasn't a kangaroo; it was just a 'roo. And the "roo bars," intended for trouble like this, hadn't done their job.

"So Jurgen says to me, 'You grab his tail and I'll grab his paws, and we'll haul him out of the goddamn way.'"

They had pushed the car into the meagre shade of a desert oak and begun a long wait. They couldn't sit down because of ants. They couldn't sit in the car for heat. The sun soon lowered itself and blasted away their shade.

Floyd sank another, then ran his hand over a meaty face. He continued: "'Tell you what,' Jurgen says to me when our beer's all gone. 'Let's get some pictures of this fella for our better halves back home.'" They grasped the dead roo by its tail, thick and limp like a bell rope and dragged it over to the car. The roo was heavier than it looked, but they managed to prop it up against the grille with its fine head lolling on its chest like a drunken girl's. Floyd took pictures of Jurgen with his arm around the narrow tawny shoulders and his baseball cap perched between the ears. The cap said: PRODUCT: LAND OF PLENTY. Jurgen took some of Floyd. Then he went to the car for his jacket—a purple nylon jacket with PRODUCT REALTY emblazoned over the pocket in orange lettering—and put it on the kangaroo. The effect, I gathered, was Peter Rabbit on heroic scale.

Floyd and Jurgen had stepped back to admire their tableau. As they did so, the victim of their humour raised its head and regarded them with dreamy eyes. Before the two could react, the kangaroo shook itself and hopped off into the desert, but the purple nylon jacket, containing Jurgen's passport and travellers' cheques, disappeared into a burning Outback sunset.

"Good thing we got the pictures." Floyd signalled for another round. "American Express might be sticky about a refund."

BY INVITATION

Max Wyman
QUEST

One summer in the early 1960s, while we were still living in England, my wife and I took a holiday in a small village on the Costa Brava. A few days before we left home, a young British couple arrived by motorbike. They seemed lively and intriguing people—we would hear them return to the hotel late at night after their nocturnal outings—and we hoped we would have the opportunity to talk with them. Unfortunately, our departure day arrived before we were able to make an introduction.

In 1967 we emigrated to Canada, and settled in Vancouver. I began to work as a reporter for the *Vancouver Sun*. There were several other young English immigrants in the *Sun* newsroom, and I struck up a friendship with one in particular, Dave Hardy. He and his wife became regular guests at our home, and we at theirs. One night when we were at their place for dinner, they pulled out their album of honeymoon pictures to show us.

They explained they had gone touring by motorbike in Spain that year—and had stayed in a tiny village on the Costa Brava. Look, said Dave, here's a picture of us in the hotel restaurant.

At a table immediately behind them sat my wife and I.

Carmen Ziolkowski

A MEMORABLE NIGHT

A person's soul is a maze of nooks and recesses to hide the hurts inflicted on it. At times a crisis bares our soul. The news of the Gulf War and the bombing of towns and villages brought to the fore a frightful happening which I experienced in January 1944.

I was barely a teenager when the war was raging in Italy. I was in boarding school in Rome, and my family lived in Naples. For over six months I had had no news from my parents.

The battlefield was moving closer to the center of Italy and nearer Rome. The director of the school decided that the responsibility for so many young girls' fate was too much for her to take. So one cold Sunday morning the students from the South of Italy were put on the train; two nuns accompanied us to deliver each one to our parents.

During wars, nothing works as planned. The train left Rome and chugged on for about seventy-five miles. It stopped at Cassino and went no further. The railway tracks had been bombed. Our chaperones were frantic and didn't know what to do with us.

We huddled in front of the station. It was full of soldiers, mostly Germans and some Italians. Scared and restless, I moved away from the group to have a smoke. As I pulled a cigarette from my purse, a young man held a light for me. I thanked him, and we began to exchange a few words. I told him about our plight.

"You are lucky to have stopped here. . . there's fighting not far away. Monte Cassino is crawling with

Germans." Then he told me his name—Savio—and I told him mine.

There was a roar in the sky, and he said, "God! Will any of us be alive tom—" A loud blast—the very pavement shook under our feet.

The boy pushed me to the ground and covered me with his body. How long we lay there I can't tell. When finally I stood, the whole place was in an uproar—the station had been hit; everyone was running helter-skelter. My protector was pressing his hands to his face. I saw blood oozing through his fingers. To my exclamation of horror he said, "It's nothing . . . you go . . . go with the nuns. I'll be fine."

And he disappeared into the night.

Other Canada India Village Aid publications:

The Dry Wells of India, edited by George Wood-cock with an introduction by Margaret Atwood, is an anthology of poems submitted to the Canadian Poetry Competition to raise funds for CIVA's drought relief project in Rajasthan. (Available from Harbour Publishing)

Walls of India, a handsomely produced account of travel in India, is vintage prose by George Woodcock and vintage painting by Toni Onley, two directors of CIVA. (Available from CIVA)

For more information on Canada India Village Aid, please write to CIVA, 5885 University Boulevard, Vancouver BC V6T 1K7.

Printed in Canada